Bunker

Andrea Maria Schenkel

Translated from the German by Anthea Bell

First published in Great Britain in 2010 by

Quercus
21 Bloomsbury Square
London
WC1A 2NS

German original, *Bunker*, first published by Edition Nautilus.

English translation Copyright © 2010 by Anthea Bell
Copyright © 2009 by Edition Nautilus

Published by agreement with Edition Nautilus.

A CIP catalogue reference for this book is available from the British Library

ISBN 978 1 84916 112 1

10 9 8 7 6 5 4 3 2 1

Designed and typeset by Lindsay Nash
Printed and bound in Great Britain by Clays Ltd, St Ives plc.

Bunker

I still have to get the keys. They're in the bedroom, on the bed. Back into the bunker. Damn, the paraffin lamps have burnt out, even though I had two for each room in it. Funny, I thought those things lasted longer. What a waste, six lamps in three rooms, and all of them gone out. Dammit! I have a torch in the car. Must be in the glove compartment, but I don't feel like going back for it. If I leave the door wide open there might be enough light from the stairway for me to see into the back room.

It's still light enough here in the front room. I'll leave the connecting door wide open. It's already quite dark in the second room. The fittings of the little kitchen counter along the wall don't reflect much of the light coming in. Pitch black in the third room. My feet come up against the plastic sack, and then I have to feel my way along the side of the bed. Why did those stupid lamps go out so quickly? I filled them, or did I forget to? Well, that won't get me anywhere now. I need those damn keys. Where are they? I left them on the bed. I feel the pillow, nothing there. The sheet under it, still nothing. OK, keep calm. Those keys just have to be here. Keep calm! Pull the quilt right down to the foot of the bed...nothing. Those bloody things must be here. I saw them, clearly! Chucked them on the bed with the rest of the stuff from the jacket. This is too much. I'll just strip off all the bedclothes. Maybe the keys will fall on the floor then... Nothing. Shit, shit, shit! Rummage through everything again – still nothing.

Where are the stupid things? Keep calm. Think about it, think. Of course, I must have knocked them under the bed. Crawl under it. Disgusting, dust and dirt all over the place. And those crumbly heaps of something. Heaps of what? Mouse shit, can only be mouse shit. This place must be teeming with mice, filthy vermin. It stinks of mouse piss down here too, and I'm lying flat on my front in all that dirt, groping about in the dark for those damn keys. I squeeze under the bed as far as I can; I can touch the wall with my fingertips now, it's all cold and slimy. No wonder the whole wall's mouldy, everything down here is damp and cold.

Dust, dirt, mouse piss, mould. This is getting me nowhere, I'll have to go and fetch the torch or nothing's going to come of this, nothing at all. I slowly begin wriggling out from under the bed again.

What's that sound? Is there someone at the door? No, can't be, who'd be there? That fat slob is dead. But there's someone tinkering about with the door. No, no! Damn it, there is someone there. Can't be her, can it? Who's there? Shit, shit! This is all going wrong! Who can that be? Just don't let me hear the door squeal now, please don't let it squeal!

Push off from the wall and crawl out from under the bed. Takes far too long. I'll do it yet, I'll make it to the door. Quick, quick! I'm scurrying on all fours, trying to stand up as I crawl, trying to get to the door. Through the second room. I can see the door! The bunker door closes slowly, very slowly. Squealing.

Darkness. I stumble, fall to the ground. My face hits the concrete – it feels hard, cold, clammy. The palms of my hands are stinging from the impact. I try to push myself up, raise my head, look at the door. It's closed. All dark around me, only that narrow strip of light under the bunker door. I crawl forward, making for the strip of light. I can hear myself breathing, taking air in noisily through my open mouth. I'm breathing fast, my ribcage rising and falling at every breath. I lie down flat on the floor in front of the strip of light. Try to get my face really close to it. I can feel the cold draught of air coming into the bunker through the gap. Maybe I can look out through it? I have to squeeze my face down on the floor even harder. Very close to the gap, right up against it. The shadow of two feet. The shadow disappears.

I hear a hollow thud; the wooden trapdoor has come down, the gap with the light showing through has gone. Total darkness. Everything's black, everything. Pitch dark every-where.

I'm still lying in front of the door. The right-hand side of my face on the cold concrete floor, mouth and nose pressed to the gap under the metal door. I'm gasping for air in panic, like a fish on dry land.

I lie there. I ought really to jump up, shout, hammer frantically on that door. But I lie there exhausted, empty. Losing any sense of time in the darkness. Feeling the cold of the concrete seeping slowly into me, feeling myself chilling. It's like falling into a dark hole. I suck air in, and with every breath I'm pulled deeper. I close my eyes, or did I just open them? Doesn't matter, the darkness is still the same. I lie there feeling drained, horribly drained.

The room is bathed in red light. I can't make out where

the light's coming from. In it I see myself getting up, slowly looking around. I'm not alone. I hear footsteps. I'm walking through this sea of red light, following the footsteps into the middle room. I see him there, a big, strong man. Hair cut very short, jeans and army jacket. He's going through the room, right to the back room of the bunker. At the back wall he stops, turns to me. I see his face, a striking nose with a dip in it, prominent cheekbones, eyes deep-set in their sockets. Eyelids drooping, expression of burning self-confidence and determination. He pushes off from the wall with one leg, strides towards the locked steel door, turns his right shoulder in that direction and rams the door with it. The door springs open with a deafening noise, glaring white light dazzles me, hurts my eyes. I put my hands up to protect my face. He must have jumped over me. I lower my hands again, carefully open my eyes.

The room is pitch black, the bunker door is closed, I'm still flat out on the cold floor in front of the door, I'm trapped in this hole underground.

A week earlier...

Friday afternoon, the evening rush hour, car after car, bumper to bumper, all the way down the street. The air is full of exhaust fumes from the vehicles, a stale smell with every breath you take. Loud traffic noise, horns honking, edgy, impatient pedestrians in amongst it all. Everyone wants to get home. A woman hurries over the road, dodging the stationary cars. Cyclists wind their way through the queuing traffic, swerving right or left wherever there's a small gap. Crowding together at the lights. One of them can't wait, rides his bike along the pavement. Pushes past the pedestrians, almost running one of them down. The man jumps out of the way just in time, shouts angrily at the cyclist. The cyclist rides on, takes no notice. I stand on the pavement watching. Cars right down both sides of the street. A line of parked vehicles adds to the traffic chaos. I look across at the car hire firm's parking place. All the vehicles are quite old models, but all washed and polished. The building the other side of the fleet of cars is concrete, large windows without any visible frames, just dark outlines where they fit into the concrete slabs. I can't see into the building through the tinted glass of the windows. A customer goes in. The glazed front door opens automatically. Through the open door I get a moment's glimpse of the interior. She's standing behind the dark wood of the reception counter.

She's busy sorting through a stack of papers. No one else in the room. The door closes, opens again a little later. She shows the customer out, gives him the car keys. I see the red tag of the keys, there's a brief exchange of words, they shake hands, the man gets into a grey BMW. She waves him out of the parking slot, smiles briefly, nods and goes back into the building.

I cross the road, winding my way through the stationary traffic like the other pedestrians. I cross the car park. The path is paved with exposed aggregate concrete slabs.

The automatic glass door opens. I go in. She's busy with her papers again. She doesn't even look up. Doesn't say a word to me. Goes on putting her papers in order, as if she were still alone in the room.

I stop at the counter. Wait, never taking my eyes off her.

'We're closing in two minutes' time.'

'I know.'

She's kneeling in front of me, her hands tied behind her back with a length of washing line round her wrists. Her back is bent so that her shoulders hunch forward. Her head is bowed, her shoulder-length dark hair hangs over her face like a curtain. I hear her breathing in and out. She takes in air, lets it out again through her tightly closed lips with a soft little hissing sound. Kneeling, she comes nearly up to my belt. I take a step back. Her breasts rise and fall with every breath. She's afraid, I can feel her fear. A small, gleaming drop of sweat runs down to her breasts. I watch the drop slowly making its way over her bare skin, disappearing down into her neckline.

With my left hand I take hold of her hair, grab it tight, jerk her head back. She utters a short scream. Damn it, I want her to look me in the face. Her eyes avoid me. She keeps staring down. Her forehead is wet with sweat, her eye make-up smeared, streaks of mascara running down her cheeks. The outlines of her face are blurred by the smudged make-up. She whimpers, sniffs, draws air noisily in through her nose.

I pull her head back again with my left hand. My right hand grabs her chin and squeezes it.

'Where's the key? Come on, where's the key?'

She sniffs snot back up her nose again. I swing back the hand that was squeezing her chin just now, hit her in the face. She moans. Even though I'm still holding her hair, her head jerks slightly to one side. The rim of one nostril turns red, a thin trail of blood runs out of her nose and down her chin. She's crying quietly.

'The key, right now!'

My left hand shakes her head back and forth. Droplets of blood fan out on my shirt. I feel disgusted. And furious. Why doesn't she say something? Why does she just keep on crying?

I clench my fist and hit her in the face once more. Her head jerks to one side again. Next moment she falls forward with her eyes closed and her mouth pursed up. She stays there propped on her shoulders for a second, then slowly shifts back to a kneeling position. I look into her face. It's ridiculous, with that pouting mouth and her eyes like slits.

'The key, or else...'

I'm kneeling in front of him, my hands tied behind my back. He's walking nervously around in front of me, his upper body moving back and forth. I try not to look at him, keep my eyes fixed on his shoes. Trainers. He's trying to be cool. Arsehole. Just don't look at him, look at his shoes, don't look him in the eye. Don't look at his face. Keep looking at his shoes. His shoes.

He grabs my hair with one hand and wrenches my head far back. Swings his arm. I feel a deep, penetrating pain, my skull seems to be splitting. That bastard, he hit me in the face! I hurt all over. My head, my shoulders, my hands and knees. That bastard, that filthy, bloody bastard! The key, or else...the key...I don't have the key!

He swings his arm back again, hits me in the face a second time. Bright lightning flashes in front of my eyes. My left eye is throbbing. I can hardly stand the pain. Like a long, sharp needle running through my skull. Going deeper every time my heart beats, deeper and deeper. I try opening my eyes. Open your eyes! For God's sake open your eyes! It's no good. I can't open them. The pain! Open your eyes! Pull yourself together, open them! The light's so bright, incredibly glaring. I can't keep my eyes open. Can't. I try again. My left eye stays closed, my right eye opens just a crack. Everything's all blurred. The hand in my hair jerks my head back. Pain again, my head is bursting.

The key...the key...I feel as if the ground's giving way under me. Heat rises in me, running up over my back, the nape of my neck, it takes hold of my head from behind, breaks over my forehead like a wave. I slowly sag and collapse, let myself fall...just let myself fall...

I fall through a never-ending black void. Suddenly there's something shining – I feel drawn to that light, it's like swimming through the void towards the light. The brightness pushes the dark away. I'm in a room. I know the room, I've been here before, I've been here countless times. Don't know when. Don't know why. I'm turning around myself, turning on my own axis. Seeing the room through my eyes, seeing myself at the same time, watching myself turning and look-ing around. The little boy appears as if out of nowhere, standing in front of me, small and skinny. I go towards him, I don't recognize him, yet he's somehow familiar to me, like the room where I find myself now. The boy's face changes, it looks more familiar with every step that I take closer to him. Joachim? Joachim, it's Joachim, it must be Joachim! My doubts change to certainty. With a girl beside him, may-be thirteen years old, dark-blonde hair in plaits. Closer, closer still. Where did that girl come from all of a sudden? She's standing in the room beside me, no, she's not beside me…I'm inside her. I'm the girl. I'm the girl, I'm a child again. The images flow into each other, each emerging from the one before it. The boy, Joachim, turns to me. I can't under-stand what he's saying. He's babbling away much too fast. I can't understand him, it makes no sense. Slowly, words form.

I'm beginning to understand him. 'Piggy bank.' I look at the floor. There are bits of broken earthenware all over it. Coins among the broken bits. Pfennigs, ten-pfennig pieces. Joachim bends down, kneels in front of me. He's wearing short trousers, kneeling on the broken piggy bank with his legs bare, his knees bleeding. He looks down at the coins. My hand takes hold of his soft hair, shakes his head, hauls it up to me, his face wet with tears. Snot running out of his nose.

'You lousy little thief!' I feel the rage in me, I feel incredible rage. My free hand keeps hitting his little head, won't stop. He's bleeding, I keep on hitting him, again and again...until his head, his body go slack, hanging from my hand. I watch myself with indifference as I let go of him. His body sags, now he's lying on the floor without moving, lying on the broken piggy bank. Blood slowly trickles from his ear in a thin red line. Curious, I put out my hand to touch the trickle of blood. See it shining on my fingertip. I bend down, feel my lips touching his cheek; I kiss his hair, all smeared with blood. Even as my lips touch him I want him to disappear. His body has to go! I must get it away! I fetch the wheel-barrow, try to heave the body into it. Even though he's so small and thin, he feels incredibly heavy. As soon as I've done it and he's in the wheelbarrow, he slips out again the other side.

'Hello, Monika, want to take me for a walk?' I stop in surprise, I turn around. I'm in a meadow, not inside a room any more. Joachim is standing there, leaning against a willow tree. Joachim who was lying on the floor like a dead body just now. He's holding one hand to his ear, grinning.

The picture blurs, I wake up from the dream, I slip back into reality. I try opening my eyes. It works only with the right eye, and even that eye not properly. I blink, the light's glaring, dazzling. I close my eye again. Try once more. This time I manage to keep it open a little longer, I'm getting used to the brightness. Where am I? Am I alone? I don't feel the hand in my hair any more. I'm lying on my side, hands still tied behind my back. My coat over me. On the fitted carpet with my back to the wall, in the corridor between the office door and the staff toilets. How is the coat arranged, where are the coat pockets? On the inside. He's put the coat over me lining side out. I try to get hold of the fabric with my fingers. Grope around as well as I can with my hands tied behind my back. My arms hurt, my hands feel as if they've gone to sleep. I have to wiggle my fingers for a little while to bring them back to life before they'll obey me. Somehow or other I manage to wedge the fabric between my fingers. I feel the edge of the coat pocket. Get hold of the inside-out edge of the fabric. Pull it towards me, little by little. The fabric slips out of my fingers. Shit! I try again. Once, twice. My pocket-knife is in there. I manage to get my fingers inside the pocket. I feel the cold metal. I must shake the knife out of the pocket. Somehow or other I must shake that damn knife out of my coat pocket. I've no idea how I'm going to do it, but I try. Again and again and again. Until I manage to get the knife wedged between my forefinger and middle finger. Slowly pull it out of the pocket. My fingers get stuck at the fabric edge of the coat pocket; I press them more tightly around the handle of the knife. The pressure makes it slip out of my fingers again, back into the coat pocket. Bloody hell.

I hear sounds, footsteps coming closer, very close. I close my eyes, pretend I'm asleep. He's standing right in front of me. I don't need to open my eyes, I know who's standing there. The toe of one shoe is pushed under my face, turns my head suddenly from lying sideways to facing up. My heart is thudding. My breath stays steady. Slowly, I open my right eye. I try to look at him. The light is behind him, so I see only his outline. His body looks massive. He has very short hair. Have I ever seen him before? Does he look familiar to me? A customer? Damn it, I can't remember.

'The key!'

Police cars, fire service vehicles, engines running, blue lights, noise, the narrow path through the forest is jam-packed with them. One after another, no way of getting through.

The forest is full of flashing light.

Outside the mill, the compressor roaring, thick cables running over to the house. Two large searchlights set up outside the metal door, lighting up the entrance to the mill. Unnaturally glaring light, the whole scene is improbable, like something on stage in a theatre. The area outside is brightly illuminated too. The old wooden door lying on the darkly gleaming swampy ground; the bushes along the path cast harsh shadows.

I got up early, packed my things, and now I'm on my way. There's no one else around yet. The newsreader on the car radio is talking about rioting and violence between neo-Nazis and police outside an immigrants' hostel in Hoyerswerda. I switch the thing off.

Mist lies above the forest. It is early morning, the mist is beginning to drift apart and dissolve until it's all disappeared. The ground is still moist with dew. The air smells of wet earth. I like it. I've wound the window down a little way, I can feel the airflow as I drive, I smell the forest.

Pine trees grow close together all the way up to the side of the road. The road divides the forest, cutting it in two. The tarmac is still wet in many places, the road surface looks dark, almost black.

Just before the sharp right bend I take my foot off the accelerator and turn left into the cart-track, reducing my speed. The place is hard to find. I drive on along the unmade track, reducing speed again. I continue almost at walking pace over gravel, avoiding the potholes left by the last heavy rain. The path gets narrower and narrower; the ride is bumpy now. There are deep ruts in the ground, a space that rises higher between them. I avoid large stones to keep the under-carriage of the car from coming down on them. The further the track leads into the forest, the more the undergrowth and bushes encroach on it. Branches brush against the car, I let it move forward very slowly. I stop at the big fir-tree root. No motor vehicles can get any further along the track.

I switch off the engine, climb out of the car and go round to the rear door. The bloody boot is stuck again, won't open. The jolting and the unmade surface of the track have tilted the old chassis out of true. I hit it with the palm of my hand. No good. I need a tool to lever the catch open. There's a screwdriver in the car. I get it out of the glove compartment, insert it under the catch of the rear door to the boot, and it springs open.

Now that it's open I take the plastic bags and my back-pack out. A bag in each hand and the backpack over my shoulders, I trudge along the overgrown forest path. The thorns of the brambles catch in my trouser legs. I take no notice, pull myself free as I walk on, try to avoid them. The path runs slightly downhill here; I go down it to the pond. Wet leaves and mossy stones make the path slippery. The pond is an artificial one, laid out long ago as a fishpond, fed by damming and diverting water from the little stream. It was supplied through a wooden spillway, but over the years that has rotted, and the pond has turned to swampy, brackish mud. It only fills up occasionally after long, heavy rainfall. In hot summers it stinks to high heaven. Then the mud turns leathery and dull, and broad cracks appear in it, scaly and smelly.

I follow the path on along the bank and over to the old mill. The millwheel is stuck in the mud of what used to be the supply to the pond, with reeds growing around it. Only a few wooden ribs still hang in the metal frame of the wheel. The house itself is still in good condition, except for the roof. Every strong wind does more damage, and soon a storm will take the whole thing off. I ought to repair it.

At some time the old wooden front door was replaced by an iron one. The old door lies outside in the mud, bridging a marshy patch of ground. I raise the iron door slightly to open it, bracing my whole weight against it. The hinges are rusty, and it's difficult to open. The room beyond is dark, the air musty and heavy with the damp. No electricity, only paraffin lamps in the house. I put the bags down on the floor and take off my backpack. I light the lamps with my cigarette lighter. I close the door.

He tied a blindfold round my eyes before pushing me into the car. I lie there with my hands bound behind my back. The toes of my shoes just touch the floor of the car. As he drove over the bumpy road the blindfold slipped. Through the narrow space, I can see the back of a car seat. The drive seems endless. But then the car stops and the door is opened.

'Come on, stand up!'

The man takes hold of my arms and legs, tries to pull me out of the car. I'm scared. What's he going to do to me? I can't get out of the car fast enough for him. He pulls my hair. Hands behind my back, legs gone to sleep. He couldn't care less, the bastard. He goes on pulling me out. I stumble, can't find my footing, try to get my hands in front of me, can't. I scream. I fall forward, can't support myself on anything, I land on my face. As I fall I turn over on my side. Leaves, fir needles, earth in my mouth, in my nose. I cough, spit stuff out, I stay lying there. Everything hurts. The cord round my hands is cutting into my flesh worse than ever. My head hurts so badly.

'Stand up!'

The bastard is shouting at me. Why doesn't he understand that I can't, not with my hands tied? I just want to stay lying on the forest floor. The ground smells good, smells of mushrooms, earth, moss. All of a sudden I feel calm, I'm not afraid any more. Let him do whatever he likes! I'm staying here on the ground. If he wants to kill me he'll have to do it here. I'll just stay lying where I am, I won't move. My life might end here and now. There's something peaceful about the idea. I feel a strange wish for it: just to stay here for ever and ever.

His hand is tugging at my shoulder. He grabs me, hauls me up. Why can't he just leave me alone? I get a bit of purchase on the ground once I'm kneeling. He pushes me in the ribs until I stand up, then forces me back to the car.

'Now, sit down! Wait!'

I try to sit down, but I slowly slip to the ground, my back against the car door. I stay squatting on the ground. I hear quiet footsteps. The car doors are opened and closed. The slight sound of footsteps again, dry twigs snapping. Then silence. Nothing happens. I wait. Why should I wait here? Why isn't anything happening? Insects humming quietly around me, that's all, a lot of birds twittering. I sit there, breathing, calming down. Nothing happens.

Am I alone? I rub my head against the car, pushing the blindfold further up. It works loose and falls off. I open my eyes as far as I can with one of them so swollen, see the irregular outline of the treetops moving slightly back and forth, rays of light from the setting sun falling through them. I sit there leaning against the car, it's warm, my body relaxes. No sign of that guy, I'm alone.

As if by some miracle, I'm still holding the little pocket-knife. I didn't drop it when I fell, I kept it clutched in my fist. I was trying to open it all through the drive. I didn't succeed. Now, sitting here with my back to the car, I try again. And this time it works. I can open the knife. A little way, then a little more. The knife jumps out of my hand and falls to the ground. Bloody hell! I grope about on the ground with my fingers. I can't find it, but I touch a squashed tin can. I rub the cords against the sharp lid of the can. I shift, it scratches my wrists, but never mind that now. Desperately I tug and pull at my bonds, until the cord comes apart and my hands are free. I shake them, rub my sore wrists. Everything is still calm around me. I cautiously look in all directions. The forest, the woodland track, the car.

Slowly, I get to my feet. I'm alone. I'm free. I can get away. I walk round the car, taking care with every step. Maybe the key's still in the ignition. I slowly press the door handle until the driver's door opens with a loud click. Hell! I stand there for a moment, drawing air in sharply through my teeth, and looking in all directions again. Thank God, still no one anywhere in sight. I open the driver's door fully, lean forward and into the car. Where's the ignition? Out of sight under the steering wheel. I put my hand through the spokes in the steering wheel and grope for the ignition, feel the longish slit.

Damn, no key.

At that moment I hear something crack behind me. Leaning half over the steering wheel, I stare straight ahead, I daren't move. I feel sweat at the back of my neck and running down my backbone. I'm still in the trap, that bastard must be behind me.

Slowly, I straighten up, duck my head as I clamber out, take a step backwards, look cautiously around. Nothing! Just the insects humming and the birds twittering, no human being.

I have to get away from here. Along the forest path, the

way he brought me in the Fiesta? He'll be sure to search that first, and with the car he's bound to catch up with me. That's no good. I must cut through the forest. Find a road or a house.

Where's he gone? Never mind. I must just get out of here before he turns up again. I force my way through the brambles and undergrowth, going further into the forest. I run, I stumble, I jump up. I have no idea where I'm going, I'm just running, running away. I see a path through the trees, it's almost overgrown. My blouse catches on thorns. I trip over a root, tear my tights, scramble up again, wipe the dirt off my knees and run on. I keep looking round, but no one's following me. The path leads along the bank of a dried-up pond. A big, black wooden house beside it. I cross an old wooden door lying over a muddy stream. The door wobbles as I cross it. I go up to the house. Its rusty iron door is open just a crack. I make my way in. Now I'm the other side of the door.

The light of the setting sun falls through the doorway into the room. Casts golden light on a narrow strip of floor and the wall beside it. The rest of the room is dimly lit. I stand there waiting. It will take my eyes some time to get used to the darkness. Slowly I start to make things out. A large room without any windows, with a low, narrow brick wall across it, beginning in the middle of one wall. My glance moves over the projection to the darkness beyond and the opposite wall. There's a closed door on the other side of the room. Part of a wooden ladder to the right, beside the door. Its top rungs emerge from an open trapdoor to the cellar below. I lean over and look down. I see large crates and thick pipes going up to the ceiling. Everything is all jumbled up. Nothing's tidy, the place looks deserted. A wooden staircase rises to my right. My eyes follow the steps up. The stairs end at another trapdoor. The back of the room is in gloom, a little light coming through from the upper storey. A bright strip around the edge of the trapdoor picks out its position on the dark ceiling.

I hear footsteps above. Someone's up there. My eyes try to follow the invisible person. The weight of his footsteps sends dust trickling through the cracks between the wooden planks in many places. Motes drifting slowly down, floating in the narrow strip of light shining through the crack of the open doorway. I look up, transfixed. Stare at the dark ceiling until my eyes hurt. A sharp burning pain makes me close them.

Who's up there? I'll have to ask if he can help me. Will he take me to a phone box, or maybe he even has a phone here? I must call the police. But suppose it's *him*? No, he'll be searching for me in his car, going back along the road. He'd think I could never be silly enough to run into the middle of the forest without knowing where I was going. But suppose it *is* him after all? There's still time to get away from here. Hell, what am I to do?

I pluck up all my courage. The bottom step of the stairs creaks when I try it. I stop, hold my breath, looking up in suspense. I wait. Nothing happens. No more footsteps up there. Silent as the grave. Did whoever's there hear me? Is that why it's so quiet?

Nonsense! Don't be so stupid! The next steps don't make any sound at all. There's a cast iron catch fitted to the underneath of the trapdoor. I hesitate for a moment, then I take hold of the catch and push the trapdoor up. It's very heavy; I push at it with my head until I can open it a crack. I peer through the gap. The legs of chairs and a table in the middle of the room, to the left an old bedstead with a faded flower pattern painted on it, to the right a chest of drawers and a wardrobe with round feet. No one in sight.

But I can only see part of the room through the crack. I raise the trapdoor further. Tilting my head back, I reach up and push it open as far as I can reach, rubbing against the rough wood, my hair snags on it. I still can't see enough, I can hardly hold the trapdoor open. I take one more step, push the door further up until my head is halfway through the opening. Now at last I can see more. I realize I'm getting out of breath. The trapdoor is pressing against the nape of my neck. The bloody thing's so heavy.

'So there you are!'

I lose my footing on the stairs. I stumble, I slip. Let go of the catch of the trapdoor, hit my head on the steps, stay lying at the foot of the stairs. Everything goes black around me.

A paramedic comes through the metal front door of the mill, which is wide open, walking backwards, carefully placing one foot behind the other. His jacket is bright red in the glaring floodlights, the reflective strips on the back of it are radiant white. Little by little, the stretcher is brought into the light. The legs of the person lying on the stretcher appear first. The paramedic at the front casts a long shadow on the body lying under the blanket.

The second paramedic appears. Nodding his head back and forth, calling instructions like 'Careful!' and 'Over to the left a bit', he guides the first paramedic out of the house, over the old wooden door lying on the ground, and along the forest track to the ambulance. The stretcher is pushed into the vehicle, the door is closed with a loud metallic bang.

I'm lying there with my eyes closed. Listening to music, soft, pleasant, especially the singer's voice. I like his husky tone. It's an oldie, I must have listened to that song thousands of times before. I start humming along softly to the tune. The quilt is wrapped around me, I feel good. I stretch, slip further under the quilt, pull it up to my eyes. It's too short, now my feet are sticking out. Not that it's cold, but covered up is more comfortable. I cross my feet and rub the sole of one over the back of the other. I clasp the toes of one foot around the toes of the other. Slowly I run my hand over my body. I'm naked!

All at once the pleasant sensations of the last few minutes are gone. I know I didn't undress myself! I open my eyes.

A stabbing pain. I see the wooden ceiling of the room, but the room itself is entirely strange to me. Where am I? Don't panic – think! The last thing I remember is the bloody trap-door…and that guy. He was standing behind it. I was scared to death, and then I don't remember any more. What happened? Did he put me on this bed? Did that man undress me, put me on the bed and cover me up?

I sit up in bed and look at the room. It's the one with the upper trapdoor leading to it. How long have I been asleep? My watch has gone as well.

I look around me.

He's sitting on the chair, arms on the table, his head buried in them. He's asleep. I draw my legs up and clasp my arms tightly around them. I crouch like that at the far end of the bed. Now what? Quick! Think! Come on, girl, do something! Fight or flight? Go on, make up your mind! I look at the trapdoor. I look round the room again. That guy has fallen asleep sitting at the table. Fast asleep, I can hear his heavy, noisy breathing.

Flight, then. But how? First I need my clothes, they must be lying around somewhere. He's fast asleep, so get moving!

Cautiously, I put the quilt back, very slowly, like in slow motion. My neck is all tense, my eye is swollen. It feels numb; I can't see properly. No sound. It bothers me, being naked. I work my way to the edge of the bed, sit on it, can't see my clothes anywhere.

I can't get out of the place like this, with nothing on. I need my blouse at least, or a towel. I can't take the quilt if I'm going to run for it, it would just get in the way. Maybe my things are in the wardrobe?

I feel for the floor with my feet, slowly stand up. Start moving cautiously. On tiptoe. The floor gives slightly under me, creaking. I stop. Oh, come on, pull yourself together, the man's dead to the world, he can't hear you! I bite my lower lip, try to stop myself panting. I walk on. When I reach the table I stop for a moment, looking down at his head. His hair is cut very short. His breath is rattling a bit; when you listen hard it's almost like snoring. He's sleeping deeply, I can do it! I go on moving cautiously towards the wardrobe. The key is in the lock. What a bit of luck! I mustn't make any noise, that's all. It's hard to turn the key. I know these old things, my parents had an ancient wardrobe like this in their bedroom. The damn thing gave me no end of trouble when I was snooping about. In time, however, practice taught me how to open it without any sound at all, you just had to put your hand against the door and push at the right moment. If you didn't do that, the mechanism sprang open with a deafening click.

I cautiously turn the key, a little more, a little more again. Crack!

Was that loud? No, it's just that I was concentrating so hard it seemed to me terribly loud.

The wardrobe door slowly swings opens. Now it's slightly ajar. I can't hear him snoring any more. I daren't move. My pulse-beat is thudding in my head. I can't tell whether the guy is still asleep or not. I stand there, rigid, listening to the booming in my head.

And I feel something behind my back, or at least I think so. Not a touch, not pain. It's his eyes. I can sense it. I'm sure that guy is staring at me the way I'm staring at the wardrobe door.

Weren't things bad enough already? I've been beaten up and kidnapped. Now I'm standing in front of him naked. I let my head sink against the wardrobe door.

I wait. Nothing happens.

Oh, hell, I'm not having him gawp at my bum any longer. This is too much! I turn around slowly, trying to protect myself from his gaze as best I can with my arms. Don't let him see how scared you are!

Our eyes meet briefly, that's all. Then, still sitting on the chair, he turns away.

'Get dressed. Your clothes are in the wardrobe.'

I can't think straight, don't know what to do. I just want to get away from here. Get out of the place somehow, get away. What am I going to do? I'd like to march over and hit him the way he hit me. I'd like to go for him with both fists. That bastard, that nutcase!

Of course, that's it! He won't be expecting me to defend myself. This is my chance. I'm not letting you finish me off, you bastard! I must think it all out very precisely, the slightest mistake and things will go wrong. So how do I start?

Keep calm. Breathe deeply, head up, keep perfectly upright as you walk towards him. Don't show any fear. Best if I walk in a very feminine way. Like a model on the catwalk, step by step, one foot in front of the other, swinging my hips. A little sexiness wouldn't be a bad idea. I hope it works, I hope I can carry it off. Although, might he attack me? Guys like him fancy that sort of thing. But at the same time it scares them. I must stop right beside him and stand there. My pussy level with his face. What will he do? I bet he'll be all confused, embarrassed, stare down at his clasped hands. I bet he'll feel uncomfortable with me so close to him, naked. He's the kind who doesn't dare do it unless you're defenceless. If I'm asleep he'll feel strong, he'll bring himself off staring at my naked body.

So now what, arsehole? I imagine him beginning to sweat,

breathing in deeply, a loud noise. I have to be quite relaxed, make him feel how I relish my superiority. I must act fast. Mustn't give him time. Move fast or it will go wrong. I'll grab his head and turn it towards me. Bury his face in my belly. Hold him so he can't breathe. Press him to me good and hard. Press with all my might until he goes blue in the face and I can't hear him breathing any more. No mercy if he whimpers and begs. He doesn't deserve any. He'll try gasping for air, try to fight back. He'll wriggle like a fish out of water. If I press hard enough he won't have a chance; I just have to hold him close to myself. And I must do it all very fast, I must take him by surprise. When he's gasping I'll force his head back with all my might and shout, 'You're not hitting me again, get it?' I can imagine his swollen face, his skin wet with sweat and flushed. He'll look at me, terrified, out of little slits of eyes. Begging for mercy.

He stands up. Goes to the trapdoor, opens it, climbs down. Ignoring me. The trapdoor closes. I'm in here alone, I hesitated too long, I'm still standing in front of the wardrobe, its door half open behind my back, both arms held protectively over my body. I let my arms fall. Go over to the bed and drop on it. I pull the quilt over me and close my eyes, stabs of pain rising from the nape of my neck to my head.

There he is again, the child behind the tree. I see the little boy before me, a skinny little boy materializing out of nothing. I go up to him, I don't know him, yet he's as familiar to me as the woodland where I find myself now. I know him by his bloodstained ear. The boy's face changes, I can't see it properly. There's something I don't like about him, it scares me. The child avoids my eyes, won't look at me, stupid brat! He waves his arms about. Making signals. What does he want? The movements calm down, begin to make more sense, lines, circles, letters. Yes, he's tracing letters in the air with one finger. Writing in the air. Secret conversations, the kind we used to have as children. Painting letters in the air, or writing them on each other's backs and then asking, 'Go on, what was that word? Guess!' OK, I'll play along. I try to concentrate. I recognize a letter Y. And then a letter C. Or is it? He shakes his head energetically, starts again. An O? He nods. Then a U. He nods again. 'YOU'. Good, on we go. He writes in the air again, fast, much too fast. I can't decipher it. He writes more letters. I can't make out the word. He loses interest in the game, turns away, runs off into the woods. Wait, wait for me! I run after him, try to follow. But there's no one to be seen in the woods any more.

The bus moves slowly towards the stop. I am the only passenger. I get up from my seat while the bus is still moving. I go down the central aisle to the front door, holding on to the pole for support. I stop by the driver, lean my back against the perspex pane. The driver doesn't see me, he's looking straight ahead, keeping his eyes on the road. The bus stops. The door opens, I get out. I'm not even outside yet, my foot is still on the last step, when the first schoolkids push their way in. They storm in noisily, satchels on their backs, bags of PE kit in their hands. Pushing, shoving, shouting. Everyone's trying to get to a seat first. The doors close behind me. I stand by the side of the road, looking in the direction of the bus. The driver is sitting there behind his steering wheel, still looking straight ahead. The bus starts, passes me very close. I cross the road and on the other side I go on along the pavement. There's no one around except for me, I'm on my own. The echo of my footsteps bothers me.

It's not daylight yet, the buildings on the housing estate are only vaguely outlined. There are lights on in some of the apartments – the windows are bright patches in the grey façades of the buildings. The street lighting is still switched on but it hardly lights up its surroundings at all. I go along the tarmac path to the apartment block where I live. Stop at the glazed front door. Put my right hand in my jacket pocket and take my key ring out. I open the door, close it again; the lock latches with a click behind me.

I take the lift, go up from the ground floor to the mezzanine floor leading to the fourth storey. From there I go up the steps to my apartment. Still with the key in my hand, I open the door of my apartment and go down the corridor to the kitchen. I keep my jacket and shoes on, as I always do – I take my jacket off only when I'm in the kitchen, then I hang it over the back of the chair. I go to the kitchen counter with its row of appliances, open the fridge door, bend down, take out the bottle of milk I opened yesterday. I get a glass out of the wall cupboard, put the glass and the bottle on the table, sit down on the chair. Take my shoes off and leave them under the table. I take the bottle and pour cold milk into the glass, putting the milk back on the table. A drop runs down from the top of the bottle over the curve of its side and ends on the table top. I sit there watching the drop. I pick up the glass, take a sip, raise my head and look out of the window.

From where I'm sitting I can see into the building opposite. Light after light is switched on. Window after window is lit up. The light goes on in the apartment in front of me as well. Always at the same time every day. There are no curtains at the windows. I see straight into the bedroom. The woman is moving about there, wearing the long T-shirt that just covers her bum. She disappears. The light goes on in the next room. I can see into her kitchen. Her cat jumps up on the window sill, stretches and lies lazily down. She comes over and strokes the cat. Moves away from the window, comes back a little later with a cup. She puts the cup on the table and sits down. My eyes follow her, follow every movement she makes. She picks up the cup, drinks, puts it down again. She reads the newspaper, drinks without looking up. The cat on the window sill gets up, stretches, and jumps lazily over to the table, gets her to pet it and disappears from my field of vision. The woman stands up too, takes the cup, puts it on the work surface behind her and leaves the room. I stay where I am, drinking milk and looking at the window, waiting. After a few minutes I see her again, back in the bedroom this time. She is naked, with a towel *wrapped around her hair. She crosses the room to the wardrobe, opens it. Now the wardrobe door hides my view of her; I can't see her again until she's dressed. She is wearing a skirt and her white blouse. She closes the wardrobe, looks around her, turns off the light and leaves the room.*

I stand up as well, go to my bedroom and throw myself on the bed.

I lie there, holding the pillow clasped to me, eyes closed. Thinking of the woman in the apartment opposite. Of her naked body, the way she walks through the room as if in slow motion. I think of her like I do every day.

I open my eyes. Sit up in the bed, look round the room. No one there. I let myself drop back and stare at the ceiling.

Nothing's changed. I'm still lying on the bed naked, covered only with a thin quilt, imprisoned in a small room in a dilapidated, deserted wooden house in the middle of the forest. I've no idea why I'm here. What does that guy want? I must do something, anything, or I'll go out of my mind. I must get out of here! Come on, do something! Get up, get dressed, try to escape, it must be possible. Pull yourself together, get out of this place. I get off the bed and go over to the cupboard. My clothes are in there, like he said. I slip them quickly on, as if someone might be watching. There's an old shaving mirror hanging from a nail over the chest of drawers, a round mirror with a red plastic frame. I look terrible. Face swollen, left eye red and bloodshot, the lower lid's already starting to turn pale mauve. The mirror, which is almost entirely clouded, makes the rest of my face look even paler in contrast. As I feel my injuries and stare at my face, the right-hand side of the mirror darkens. A head comes into view over my shoulder. His head. His forehead bulges just above his eyes, which are deep-set. His nose is large and hooked, flat at the end. A deep dip in it, so that the end juts like a little triangle. The way that nose looks, he must have broken it at some time. Doesn't surprise me, a thug like that. Narrow lips above his protruding chin, which has a cleft in it.

'Hungry?'

I look into his eyes. Murky brown eyes. I hold his gaze. He smiles, a broad smile, showing his teeth. Discoloured yellow teeth with gaps in them.

'Mmm.'

I can't get any more out, just 'Mmm'. And I nod. He goes over to the table, tips the contents of a plastic bag out on it. Assorted rolls, half a loaf of dark rye bread, pretzels. From another bag he produces butter and a packet of sliced sausage wrapped in paper. He takes the slices apart with his fingers and puts them on a plate. Then several bottles of beer, standing them neatly side by side. Putting out the sausage with dirty, unwashed fingers, drinking beer, of course, just the sort of thing he'd do.

He grunts, lights a camping stove. He'd already taken it out of his backpack. He's really made himself at home here. Now he produces a pan as well. Fries eggs.

'Like some?'

'Mmm.' I won't really like anything you give me, but I'm feeling quite ill with hunger, my stomach's rumbling. Hesitantly, I sit down at the table.

'Why am I here?'

He puts the pan of fried eggs down in front of me.

'Eat it!'

'What do you want me for? Why am I here, for God's sake? Talk to me!' My voice cracks, sounds oddly squashed. Tears come into my eyes. I don't want the bloody fried eggs any more, I put my arm back ready to sweep the pan off the table. He grabs my arm, forces it down on the table.

'Eat it!'

He slowly relaxes his grip and lets my arm go. Inside me, feelings of helplessness, rage and fear are competing with each other. I start eating. First slowly, reluctantly, then faster. Rapidly. I stuff myself, eat the whole pan of eggs greedily. I mop up what's left with bread. There are tears running down my cheeks. I wipe them away with the back of my hand.

He is sitting beside me, watching me, doesn't say a word. After he's finished several beers, he stands up, clears away the crockery and the camping stove, puts it all in a wooden crate.

'Going to wash these things up. The only water's outside.'

He opens the trapdoor, climbs down the steep stairs. The door latches behind him. Creaking sounds, then silence. I hope he falls downstairs and breaks his neck.

A fly gets to work on what's left of the breadcrumbs on the table. It crawls back and forth, carefully cleaning its feelers and its face. Buzzes over to the window and then back to the table, settles on my hand. Normally I'd hit it, kill it, today it's a welcome diversion.

It must be at least an hour since he left.

I have to get out of here! I go over to the trapdoor. It's either jammed or locked; I tug until my fingers hurt. That bastard has locked me in! He's keeping me prisoner. Like an animal, he feeds me so I won't die on him. The arsehole!

I get to work on the crack around the edges of the door, levering with a kitchen knife he left up here until the blade breaks off. I'm an idiot, I might yet have used that knife as a weapon.

It's quiet in this room, all I can hear is the fly buzzing as it moves from side to side at the bottom of the window frame. Now and then, with a tiny thud, it collides with the glass and runs up and down the pane.

I go over to the window, shake it, it won't open. Clouds are slowly moving past. I stand on the chair; I can just see the treetops of the forest – they're conifers. I could break the pane, but I think better of that one at once. The window is too narrow. I couldn't get through it.

I search the room again. It's pointless, but there must be something I could use to break the door down. I haven't yet looked inside the chest of drawers. Teabags, dustpan and an ancient brush, newspaper, a small photograph frame. I have a photo frame like that at home, wood painted black, just the same. Curiously, I pick up the photograph frame, take it out, turn it over.

And stare at the picture, bewildered. This is impossible. It's a photo of me as a schoolgirl. Joachim is beside me. Joachim with his round childish face is grinning at me. I don't want to see the picture, I throw the photo frame back into the chest of drawers. How does it come to be here? It was in my bookcase, to the right of the top shelf, jammed into the corner between the wall and a row of books. So firmly jammed that you could hardly pull it out. I don't remember noticing that it was missing. Well, all my old books are on that shelf. Everything I don't want to throw out for some kind of sentimental reason. I ought to have chucked it all into the garbage ages ago.

Hesitantly, I take the picture out of the chest of drawers once more and stare at the photo as if turned to stone. There I stand, holding it in both hands. I stare at it for ever. It's already dark outside. I look at the picture until the faces in it blur, I can hardly see anything there. 'He isn't going to come back!' I jump, startled by the sound of my own voice. 'He isn't going to come back!' I say it again in an undertone, speaking to myself. I don't know which of them I mean, Joachim or my kidnapper. I cross the twilit room to the bed.

Lying on the bed, I keep nodding off, then waking with a start, then dropping off to sleep again. I don't want to sleep, I want to stay awake. I'm afraid of my dreams.

And once again I'm sucked up by a black emptiness, drawn into the void. I see a light far away, like a light at the end of a tunnel. I run towards it. The light gets larger, brighter, it pushes the darkness away. I'm in a room, I know it. I know I'm dreaming the same dream again. Again and again. And once more I'm turning on my own axis, but at the same moment I'm watching myself turning. Suddenly the little boy's there in front of me again. I go towards him. There's a warm feeling inside me, I want to hug him, I want to protect him. The little boy looks at me. He's Joachim. I glance up, and I'm looking into a mirror. I see Joachim, and I'm standing beside him, a head taller than he is. I'm thirteen years old, with long dark-blonde plaits. Joachim looks up at me, talking away to himself. He's talking much too fast. I can't make out what he's saying. It makes no sense. Only slowly do I begin to understand him.

'Piggy bank.' He's holding the piggy bank, showing it to me. I want to take it, but he sweeps his arm back and throws the piggy bank at the mirror. Our reflection breaks into a thousand pieces. They're lying everywhere, the floor is covered with sparkling broken glass. Coins among the broken glass, pfennigs, ten-pfennig pieces. I grab him, I throw him to the floor as hard as I can. Joachim is lying among the glittering splinters of glass, the light is refracted from them a thousand times. His legs are bleeding, he's crying. I look at his face, which is wet with tears. Snot running out of his nose. 'You little bastard!' I feel the fury in me, that terrible fury. I begin hitting and kicking him. I go on and on. He's bleeding, I go on hitting him, hitting and hitting...until his little body lies on the floor without moving. Blood trickles slowly out of his ear, a thin thread of blood. I put my hand out, touch the little trickle. See it shining on my fingertip. I bend down, kiss him and pet him. And at the same moment

I want him not to be there. He must go! I fetch the wheel-barrow, try to heave his body into it. It doesn't work, he falls out on the other side again and again. I take hold of his legs, see his shoes. Child's shoes. Blue fabric shoes with striped blue and white laces. Joachim's favourite shoes.

'Hello, Monika, what are you doing to me?' I stop. I turn around. I'm standing in a park. Joachim is beside me, lean-ing against a willow tree. Joachim who was lying dead on the floor only just now. He's holding one hand to his ear, grinning.

I'm sitting on one of the old wooden crates. My hunting knife in one hand, a piece of wood in the other. I hear footsteps above me now and then – she's walking up and down. I look at the ceiling. My eyes follow her invisible form. Dust sifts through the cracks between the wooden planks here and there. I watch the motes of dust drifting slowly to the floor.

I like to sit down here most of all. Among all the dusty old crates and machines. My favourite place. It always was my favourite place to play here in Father's mill. I could crawl into the old blowing engine once used to fill the sacks with flour; I just fitted through the open ventilation hatch. I had candles inside, little tea lights. Father didn't like that, he was afraid I'd set the whole mill on fire. I played engine drivers;

it was dark outside, a night journey. I could see all the instruments by the light of the candles: pressure gauge for the boiler, oil level indicator, speedometer, temperature gauge.

There were treasures in all those crates. I knew what they contained, every item. I had weapons, lots of weapons. Particularly swords, knives, guns and pistols. I needed them, too. I had to defend my mill. Against pirates and robbers. There were enemies lurking everywhere. Especially down in the bunker, where I wasn't allowed. Father had forbidden me to go there. On pain of punishment. All the same, I kept secretly peering under the wooden trapdoor, and I saw the slippery steps. The light of my candles wasn't strong enough to show me the door to the bunker; I could only guess at it. But I knew my enemies were there. They never showed themselves, they always stayed in hiding, but I was ready for them.

I'm sitting on the big wooden crate looking up. She's walking up and down. Walking up and down like Mother. Father was always locking Mother in. She'd be up there every few weeks. What she'd done wrong I didn't know, and I didn't dare ask. Father was sure to be in the right. Father was always in the right. Now and then I heard Father and Mother quarrelling, shouting at each other. I always put my hands over my ears then and sang at the top of my voice so

I didn't have to listen. Maybe Mother didn't even mind him locking her in up there. Then at least he couldn't hit her.

When Mother was locked in upstairs I could play great games. All day and all night. Father always went away then, and when he did come back, days later, he was drunk. Sometimes Mother shouted after Father. 'Unlock the door, please! Please unlock the door!' Sometimes she called for me too. Then I always kept very quiet and made out I wasn't there. I crept into the blowing engine and played engine drivers. I didn't want to hear her, I couldn't help her. Father was in the right. He was always in the right.

It's some time now since I heard any footsteps up there. The place is quiet. I steal carefully upstairs, unbolt the trap-door and open it. She's lying on the bed, quite calm. Eyes closed. She's breathing heavily, fast asleep. I go over to the bed. There she lies, holding the photo in her hands. I don't want that – I don't want her having the picture. I take it away from her. Pull it very carefully out of her hands. She doesn't notice, she goes on sleeping.

I take the quilt and cover her up. I don't want her getting cold.

I slept badly. Nightmares. It's dark in here, only the moon shining in a little. But that way at least there's some light in the room. I can just make out the shapes of the furniture. Yesterday there were still paraffin lamps here. Where's the picture? I was holding it when I went to sleep. I know that perfectly well, I'm not stupid. He covered me up, like yesterday. That's weird. I'm shivering in spite of the quilt. No one in the room apart from me. I can't understand what he wants me for. At first I thought he just wanted the money, but not another word about the money or the keys, not since we've been here. Odd. My thoughts are going round in circles. After a while I go to sleep again.

It's twilight. All of a sudden I'm wide awake. I need to

go to the toilet. I haven't been all day. I can hardly hold it in any longer. I knock, I lie on the floor and call through the crack around the trapdoor: 'Hello, I need the toilet, I have to go, it's urgent!' Nothing, he doesn't stir. 'I'll go in this room if you don't open the door!'

Nothing, not a sound, all's quiet. The pressure in my bladder is getting worse and worse. If I don't get to a toilet right away I'll wet my knickers like a little kid. 'Hey, you down there, open up! Don't you hear me? I need the toilet!'

That bastard isn't listening. I hop from leg to leg, it doesn't help. I cross my legs, bend double. 'Can't you hear me? I need a toilet. Or a bucket!' I search the place for something to go in. Nothing. Wait, the plastic bag! The plastic bag in the chest of drawers comes to my rescue. I pick up the bag and go to the farthest corner of the room. Would it be a good idea to undress completely? There's no clean underwear to put on. No time now. I pull my skirt up, take my panties right down and squat, holding the bag under me. No, this isn't going to work. If anyone could see me now they'd die laughing. I feel more like crying. I'm going to pee any moment now, and then it'll all be in the room, no rag to wipe it up, no bucket of water. I fold the top edge of the bag over until it will stand on the floor by itself. That's better. Squat low, and there we are. Sudden relief, oh, that feels good. To think something so simple can make you feel happy. Now, tie the top of the bag together, push it under the chest of drawers, done it.

Exhausted, I lie down on the bed.

How did that picture of Joachim and me get here? What does this guy want? Why did he bring me here? I don't understand any of it. I rack my brains. There's no sense in it, none at all. Think. Right. This weird character must have stolen it and brought it here, can't be anyone else. He must have broken into my apartment. But why? He didn't take anything but the picture. Or at least I didn't notice anything missing. I can't remember finding money or anything valuable gone.

But why that picture? Why would anyone go to the trouble of breaking in and stealing just a single object, a picture of me and my little brother? Any reasonable person would steal something more valuable. My stereo system, my colour TV, money, jewellery, how should I know what? If it was a bit of me he wanted he'd have taken something else. Like underclothes. I once read how Japanese like that sort of thing, they steal used underwear. Of course if he'd taken only one or two items I wouldn't have noticed. Clean or dirty underwear, whatever. I don't spend my time counting my pairs of knickers, after all.

But why a picture with Joachim in it? I had my new jeans on in that photo, my first really tight jeans. I got into a hot bath in those jeans, on purpose, to shrink them so they'd be a skin-tight fit. After that I always had to lie on the floor to get the zip done up. Wow, was I proud of them! Hair in a ponytail, dark glasses and a pouting mouth. Just like Brigitte Bardot. All her films were on TV at the time. In black and white. No colour TV then, or at least we didn't have it at home. My girlfriends stared at me, open-mouthed in envy when they saw my new look. The boys too, of course. The really cool characters had bikes with ape-hanger handlebars, banana saddles and a fox-tail blowing in the wind. The height of fashion at the time. Our contact with boys consisted of hair-pulling, spraying each other with water and teasing, but all the same we all knew what the others were doing. The others were the boys from the village school. They were always out and about on their bikes from morning to evening. The photo with Joachim was taken on a cycling trip. One of my girlfriends had a camera from a branch of Photo Porst. I remember it very well. The camera cost ten marks at the time, a cheap one, but to us that was a lot of money. And as usual I had Joachim tagging along with me. I had to take the silly little brat everywhere, he was a real pain in the neck. I was never on my own, he was always hanging on. Clinging like a burr. He used to eavesdrop on the rest of us and tell tales at home. How that little snoop got on my nerves! In the photo he was wearing those nasty pale blue canvas shoes with the striped laces. I'll never forget them! And the way he whined. 'Can't go any further!' 'Want a rest!' 'Want a drink!' Then, when I gave in to him and we went into the café on the allotments – what did it call itself? The Sunlit Land or something like that – I'd found there were only fifteen pfennigs in my purse. And that little horror pretending he didn't know anything about it. He squirmed and screeched like mad. Everyone was looking at us. A man got up from the next table and came over to tell me off. Until I took Joachim's purse out of his trouser pocket and found my five marks fifty in it! That little thief! It wasn't the first time he'd done it, but this time I'd caught him in the act.

So why the picture? Does this guy know me from the past, from my childhood? Or Joachim? I've no idea.

I lie here, far away in my thoughts. I'm thinking of the village, the meadows in summer. Lush grass, knee-high. I can remember the warm wind, and how I ran over the fields with my dress blowing in the breeze and my plaits dancing. If I close my eyes I can still feel the warm sunlight on my face. I run and dance over the soft green until I'm out of breath. Hands propped on my bare knees, I breathe deeply in and out. I have the smell of the newly mown grass in my nostrils. Its aroma is green and earthy. I'd like to stay in that lovely meadow.

I'm brought abruptly out of my memories by the creaking of the floorboards. I keep my eyes closed and pretend to be asleep. Even a daydream is better than the reality. I hear steps in the room, and the trapdoor falling into place with a thud. Only now do I open my eyes and sit up in bed. There's food and drink on the table. Oh, how thoughtful, he's taken away the plastic bag full of my pee and left a new one on the chest of drawers!

After I've eaten I'm bored again. I'm slowly losing any sense of time. I haven't washed for ages. My teeth feel coated when I run my tongue over them. I expect I'm beginning to get smelly. How long have I been here? I sleep, wake up, eat, doze gently, go to sleep again. The sky is cloudy, it never gets really light in this room. The paraffin lamps are still here, but he hasn't lit them again, and there are no matches to be found. I've looked everywhere. He probably doesn't trust me with fire. Any more than he trusts me with soap and water. But at least he's leaving me alone.

The hospital reception area has neon strip-lighting. The light is cold and glaring. Through the frosted glass panes of Accident and Emergency, the blue light of the ambulance shows as a blurred beam regularly flashing. The two halves of the big glazed door open automatically and slide apart without a sound.

Noise, footsteps, calls.

The paramedics hurry in with the injured victim, moving fast, pushing the stretcher ahead of them down the corridor.

Nurses and orderlies hurry to meet them, take the stretcher. One glance and they see how serious the situation is. Everything happens quickly, without a word. The stretcher is pushed into the resuscitation unit.

I sit on the bench in the children's playground opposite the sandbox, waiting. I can see the entrance of the building from here without being seen myself. She's punctual. As usual, she leaves the apartment block at eight-thirty in the morning. And she's wearing the beige coat that she wears every day. Bag over her shoulder. Hand around its leather straps. She goes along the path past the playground to the bus stop. I duck slightly. Head lowered, looking at my trainers. I don't want her seeing me, don't want her to notice me. She passes me and I watch her go. I see her walking past the refuse bins in the direction of the bus stop.

I stand up, follow her, an old newspaper in my hand. I stop level with the refuse bins, open the lid of one of them, throw the newspaper in. I wait. Peering out from behind the open lid of the bin. I see the bus coming closer, stopping – she gets in. The bus drives on. I close the lid of the bin and go back to her apartment block.

At random, I press one of the many bells. At the third attempt I'm lucky and I hear the hum of a door opener. I brace myself against the door, it opens, and I'm inside.

The hall of this building is hardly any different from the hall of my own opposite. The only difference is that instead of the green line running around the walls about a metre above the floor, the line here is red.

I take the lift up to the mezzanine floor leading to the fourth storey and climb the few steps up. I tread on them carefully, trying to make as little sound as possible each time I put my foot down.

I put my hand in the pocket of my army jacket and take out a small plastic card, which I insert in the groove between the door and the door frame. I bring it down a little way until it meets resistance. Take it a very little way out and then press against the latch, level with where I felt the resistance. A click and the door is open.

I look in all directions. Nothing. I disappear into the apartment.

In the corridor I stand behind the door, breathing deeply, my heart thumping. Crazy and ridiculous. This isn't the first time

I've broken into a place, yet this time it's different. I don't want to steal anything, I just want to look around.

The apartment is like my own, except that it's a mirror image. In the corridor a coat-stand with coats, a jacket, a pair of shoes on the floor. A mirror opposite. A pinboard on the wall. Cards for the theatre and concerts. I look at them more closely. Musicals, straight plays, The Phantom of the Opera, Cats, Starlight Express, Die Fledermaus *and Richard Clayderman. Not my kind of thing.*

I reach for one of the shoes and pick it up. A light brown leather shoe, the toe pointed, the brown insole slightly worn around the heel area. The heel itself is medium high, slender, slightly trodden down on the outside. I sniff it: a pleasant leather smell. When I was a child I always used to go to the cobbler's with my mother. His whole shop smelled of leather and cobbler's glue. My mother said you got addicted to that smell.

To the left, the door to her living room, no, the bathroom. Only logical, it's all a mirror image of mine. Small bottles, tubes and pots all over, under the mirror, on the glass shelf. I spray some of her perfume in the air, smells good, delicious. Clothes for washing dumped in the bathtub. I poke around in them a little. Blouses, tights, panties, a bra. I hold it up. Flesh-coloured, not at all sexy.

I go into the living room: three-piece suite, green cord cov-

ers, smoked glass coffee table. A shelving unit on the opposite wall, pale pine. I take a good look at the things on the shelves. Romances, cookery books, reference books, Yoga for Everyone, self-help manuals and a guide to the opera. In the top row, right in the back corner, something is jammed between the books and the side of the shelf. It looks like a picture frame. I reach up, take hold of the frame and pull it out. A photograph, colours yellowing a bit with age. I like the picture; it reminds me of my childhood. My mother was only a few years older than the girl in the picture when she fell pregnant. The same dark-blonde hair, the pale face. She was so slender and fragile. I take the picture with me, put it in my jacket pocket. She'll never notice.

Suddenly there's a rustling sound behind me. Quite soft. Then a scraping. I stand perfectly still, listening. I don't move from the spot. The sound gets louder. Where does it come from? The door? Damn it, she lives on her own. No one lives here except her. I open my jacket a little way and reach into the back right pocket of my trousers. I take my hunting knife out. It clicks softly as I open it. With the open knife in my hand, I steal out of the room on tiptoe and cross the corridor. The sound comes from the kitchen. Knife in my right hand, I push the door gently with my left hand. The door is ajar. It slowly opens. I take a step forward, look around. No one there.

A loud clatter, followed by a clinking sound. I spin round,

the knife still in my hand. Then I see the cat, standing on the table and hissing, its fur on end. It jumps down, races past me through the open door. Broken china on the floor. Bloody animal, how it scared me!

I close the knife, put it back in my trouser pocket. Go down the corridor to the front door of the apartment. Look through the spy hole. No one outside. I leave the apartment.

I'm bored to death. I walk up and down, climb on the chair, look at the sky and the treetops, lie down on the bed. The sky is getting darker and darker, it's beginning to rain. The rain patters down hard on the roof. I hear the water flowing away along the gutter on the side of the house. I imagine the single drops falling on the tiles, running down, collecting, forming a little rivulet, splashing into the gutter and into the downpipe. Hurrying down the side of the house into the water butt. I lie on the bed, and in my mind I follow every single drop on its way. Roof, gutter, downpipe. Again and again, roof, gutter, downpipe.

And suddenly my mind goes back to that photo, to Joachim and the way he's grinning at me in it. Who knew him? No one alive now. Our stepmother died years ago. I took the photo when I had to clear her place out, along with some other sentimental stuff. Joachim didn't have any friends. Or not real friends. He was always tagging along after me. Sticking to me like a burr. And he used to go around with Hans, the two of them spent a lot of time together. Hans the village idiot. You're not supposed to say that kind of thing these days, but it was perfectly normal at the time. Every village had its idiot, a village idiot was supposed to bring luck. The way Hans walked, the way he talked, everything about him was slow. He was retarded. Apparently he didn't even make it to special school. Hans was shapeless; a massive body, big clumsy hands, everything about him seemed to me huge at the time. Perhaps because his clothes were always too small for him. The bottoms of his trousers flapped around his shins, and of course his shirt-sleeves were too short as well. He always wore a grubby vest under his shirt. In fact the whole idea of washing was foreign to him. His body wasn't misshapen, but his shabby old clothes always made him look funny. His parents were from the East. Belorussians or something like that, I've no idea exactly what, and it never interested me. Anyway, Hans didn't speak German properly. However, he wanted to belong, and he did all he could to be one of us.

We always had a lot of fun with him. We'd egg him on to do all sorts of silly things. Like the time when we made him steal a pig for us from the biggest farmer in the village. It was one of the tests of courage we set him. He'd never have thought up the idea by himself, he was far too guileless. It didn't take us long to persuade him. Hans was strong, stronger than any of us. I can still see him grabbing hold of that pig, a young one, it struggled like mad. Hans had it in a firm grasp, both arms around it. Its hind legs were hanging down, getting in Hans's way as he tried to make off with it. But he didn't mind. He didn't let go of the pig however it twisted and turned. None of the rest of us could have caught it and taken it away like that. Not even two or three of us together. Part of the test was to throw it into the well. He actually did it, too. The pig squealed with fear, and we fell about laughing. You could hear it all over the place. Its squeals alerted the whole village. The volunteer firefighters pulled it out again. And Hans got all the blame. He didn't have to do what we said, they told him. He should have said no, he was a real fool.

Then his father beat him, beat him black and blue. He was always hitting him, he beat him almost every day. It was normal, Hans never defended himself. He just stood there and took it.

But the way he behaved to us could be unpredictable; he sometimes lost his temper. And then nothing and no one was safe. Just a small spark could do it, but once he got really worked up he'd flatten everything in his path like a steamroller.

He left Gerold in a real mess. Big-mouthed Gerold, Gerold the show-off. Today he works in the savings bank, he's turned all serious. It suits him. He was just the opposite of Hans: small, quick as a weasel, a real joker, a jack of all trades. And full of nasty digs. He used to pester Hans more than any of the rest of us.

It was Gerold who started the rumour about Hans having it off with that little boy. No idea whether there was anything in it. Gerold kept on and on at Hans, needling him all the time. Maybe Gerold wasn't so wide of the mark with his suspicions, because Hans had problems with girls anyway. So it would make sense if he fancied little boys. He couldn't just sweat it out, could he?

'Suppose Hans ever does find a dimwit to marry him, what will he ask her on the wedding night?' This was one of Gerold's favourite jokes. 'Guess! Come on, it's obvious: How many little brothers do you have?' And Gerold always roared with laughter at his own joke. We laughed as well, not because we thought it was particularly funny, but we were all glad Gerold wasn't cracking jokes at our expense.

Hans didn't laugh – he chased Gerold all round the village. He caught up with him at the Huber farm and laid into him. We stood there watching, doing nothing. If Farmer Huber hadn't come along, who knows, maybe Hans would have killed Gerold, he was in such a rage. At first even Farmer Huber couldn't separate them. Gerold was screeching blue murder. Like a sow being slaughtered. Then Farmer Huber went over to his tractor, because there was no other way to deal with it. He separated the two of them by taking Hans's head in the hay grab. Everything happened quite fast then. Hans was in such a fury that he never even noticed Farmer Huber driving up on the tractor. Somehow or other he got Hans's head lined up, tightened the grab and began lifting until Hans was hanging half a metre above the ground. But Hans still had Gerold in a headlock. He wasn't going to let him go, he never let anyone go once he had the better of him. However, this time, finally, he had to. Even Hans didn't have that much strength. Gerold landed on the ground like a ripe plum, breaking his leg. Hans raged and swore, clinging to the hay grab with both hands. Then Huber dropped him in the water of the pond the firefighters used for extinguishing fires. The grab had left two long wounds, one each side of Hans's head; they were bleeding copiously, but he took no notice. He calmed down quickly in the water, splashed out like a small child paddling, happy to be the centre of attention. And we all stood around the pond gaping. Hans put the whole incident behind him, as if nothing at all had happened. He just had those two scars on the right and left of his head. He looked funny, but then he always did. He suffered no worse damage. Very likely there was only straw inside his head anyway.

Keep still, you stupid animal! Don't struggle like that. Take it easy, take it easy, my beauty. The rabbit is lying on my right forearm, I'm holding its front paws firmly. I press its back paws slightly against myself with my elbow. My left hand is stroking its head, very gently. I run my fingers along the outer rim of its ears. From its head back to the tip of the ears. I do that several times. At first the rabbit laid them back in alarm, then it relaxed them, and they're slowly standing up as I gently pull them.

That's right, my little one, my pretty.

Rabbits are beautiful. Their fur is like human hair. They don't get on my nerves, they don't scratch or bark. They nestle against you, all soft and warm.

My first rabbit, Cuddles, was the prettiest of all. Maybe because he was my first. Maybe because I got him after Mother was gone.

I don't know what breed he was. He was mine, he belonged to me and no one else. He always listened to me. There wasn't anyone else who listened to me. He could come into bed with me in the evening, although he often made a mess there, but I didn't mind. And Father didn't mind. Keeping clean wasn't in his line. Specially not now we were on our own. He got tight almost every evening, lying on the sofa dead drunk. He stank, lay in his own filth, sometimes he even wet himself. Or he went down and shut himself in the bunker.

Father gave me Cuddles for my eighth birthday. No one had remembered my birthday, no present, no cake, no candles. Well, there wasn't anyone around to think of it by then.

'Sorry, forgot again, but I have so much on my mind.' That's what he always said when it came to giving presents. But on my eighth birthday he went into the stable, and when he came back he was holding a little ball of fluffy fur. It was soft and smelled nice. It was really cuddly, I thought, so I called my rabbit Cuddles.

Two years later Father came along, picked up the rabbit by the scruff of his neck and said, 'Well, his time's come or he won't taste good any more. Come along, you can watch!'

I didn't say anything. I knew it was going to happen. Cuddles was my friend, and Father was going to kill him.

The old threshing flail was leaning against the wall. I can see it still before me, leaning there against the wall, all dusty. Hadn't been used for ages. I wanted to pick it up and hit Father over the head with it. But I stood there rooted to the spot, couldn't move. Stood there and watched.

Keep still, you stupid creature. Keep still, sweetie. I hold the rabbit by its ears. The side of my hand comes down on the nape of its neck. A moment's twitching and then it hangs limp and still. Now to open the main artery, skin it, gut it. There we are.

The anaesthetist is summoned. He discusses the case with the duty surgeon. Everything goes smoothly, with few words, a matter of routine. All the theatre team are in their places, know what they have to do.

The patient's dirty outer clothing is cut away. A tourniquet is applied to the upper arm. Veins stand out. The injection site is dabbed with alcohol. A cannula is introduced into the vein through the skin. The metal trocar that inserted it begins to be withdrawn with a slight twist while the catheter that had surrounded it stays in the vein. The trocar is removed entirely. Blood runs out of the self-retaining cannula, showing that it is functioning properly. The infusion tube is connected, an infusion solution drips quickly into the injured patient's bloodstream.

Meanwhile the patient's head is laid right back, the mouth is opened, the intubation spatula inserted. The spatula moves the tongue aside, raises the flap over the larynx. Now there is a good view of the larynx itself, the tube is inserted into the windpipe through the vocal cords and secured there. The respiratory tube is placed on the tube already in place. Now linked to the anaesthetic apparatus, the patient is no longer breathing independently. The machine ensures deep, regular breathing.

Meanwhile the surgeon has been examining the now naked body. He removes the last compresses still lying on the patient's injuries. The large wound in the stomach comes into view. Encrusted with congealed blood everywhere. The doctor carefully separates the edges of the wound with his hands. Yellowish-white fat cells, gleaming tissue in between – good God, what a mess! The abdominal cavity is opened up. This is going to be a major operation.

It's suddenly quiet in the room. The rain has stopped drumming on the roof. I get up, go over to the window, look out. The sky has cleared slightly. The glass pane is clouded, the putty brittle. Out of sheer boredom, I try scraping the putty out of the frame with my fingernails, little by little. The window is an old double-glazed one. There were windows like that in my grandmother's house. You could open them in the middle to clean the outside. A little hook above and below, unhook the halves and they came apart. Once they were open like that, you always found ladybirds inside them towards the end of winter, waiting there for spring and sheltered from the cold. I give up and go back to the bed, simply let myself drop backwards on the mattress, bounce for a moment and lie there. I stare at the ceiling. After a while I sit up, drawing up my knees, legs pressed close to my upper body, and my thighs clasped in my arms. I begin humming to myself, rocking my torso in time, and several minutes pass before I notice what I'm doing. I immediately think of the monkeys in the zoo, sitting behind glass and rocking back and forth, or the big cats in their enclosures prowling up and down all day, up and down again and again. When am I going to start pacing up and down this room? I stop rocking, stretch my legs out straight again, prop myself on the bed with my elbows. Half sitting, half lying, I look around me, look at the floor, the bed, until my gaze finally stops at my toenails. My toenails are painted red. Were painted red. The varnish is already cracking at the edges. A little red varnish is left on my two big toes. The left toe more than the right toe. Do I step harder on my right foot than my left foot? Or why has the varnish suffered more here? Perhaps my shoe is a little tighter on that foot. The edges of the red marks are jagged, the colour is bright red. Too bright. Looks kind of cheap. And cracking too! Sloppy. Not like me at all. A darker shade of red would suit me better. I'll have to get a different nail varnish.

My fingernails look disgusting too. There are dark rims just under the nails. I get the knife off the table, sit on the bed again. Sitting cross-legged, I try to clean the dark brown dirt out of my nails with the broken kitchen knife and scrape the remains of varnish off. That works quite well. If I use the sharp, broken edges of the knife, the varnish comes off easily, flaking away in little bits. I work on my toenails until my feet go to sleep and there are little splinters of red varnish all over the sheet. Now what am I going to do with the knife? There's no water to wash it. I tug the far end of the sheet out from under the mattress and wipe the knife on it. Looks clean enough. I sniff it; there's that typical dirt-under-the-nails smell. Disgusted, I push the knife under the bed.

Food's on the table, like yesterday. No rolls this time, just four slices of dark rye bread. Not even fresh. Some kind of sausage, a bit of cheese. The milk smells fresh, a whole litre of it. I suppose these are my rations for the day. Not enough for a whole day! But who's interested? I push the plate back and forth with my fingertips. I don't have any appetite. Maybe later.

The fat fly is crawling over the table. Goes a little way, stops, goes on, stops again, cleans itself, moves on. Its proboscis gropes over the top of the table until it finds a breadcrumb. Starts in on the breadcrumb. I put my face as close to the fly as I can. The thickened end of its proboscis looks like a pair of lips. It gets the lips above the crumb. Do flies have lips? It keeps taking its proboscis away and then reaching it out again. It doesn't seem in the least bothered by me watching it, putting my face so close. It's shut up in this room just like me, it's my fellow prisoner. Hi, fellow prisoner! How can we get out of here? You could fly through the window pane if I broke it, but I couldn't. My fellow prisoner has six legs, a hairy black body and huge eyes. As far as I can remember from biology lessons, they're compound eyes, with facets. It sees everything a thousand times over with them, or maybe not quite that many. I was never too good at biology. It's a restless little thing. It leaves its bread-crumb and flies across the room. Settles on the ceiling, runs a little way along it. Takes off, comes down on the table again. Starts cleaning itself. One of the fly's front legs keeps passing over its eyes. It's a jerky sort of movement. Can flies move their eyes, maybe in different directions, like a chameleon? Now it's unfolding one of its wings. As it does that it puts out one leg, so now it's standing on only five legs, and then it puts out another. The little thing moves really well. After that it takes off again. Comes down on my arm. With a tiny, barely perceptible movement I shake it off. It's not going to be shaken off, comes back to settle on my arm again. Persistent, aren't you? I keep still, feel the touch of its little legs on my skin, a very light touch. It feels my skin with its proboscis, licking up the saltiness. That tickles. You're getting on my nerves, little fellow prisoner. I shoo it away, flapping my arms and hands back and forth. It's not bothered, it keeps coming back, even settles on my face. Oh no, you don't, my friend! It takes off again, flying on its rounds. I pick up the towel and swipe at the empty air several times. Like an idiot, I follow the fly through the room, swinging the towel wildly. I knock over the carton; milk runs out and spills over the table. By the time I can set it upright half the contents are lost. A large white puddle on the table, slowly widening towards the edge. Finally it runs over the edge of the table, a thin stream of milk running down to the floor. 'You just wait, you brute!' The fly crawls through the puddle of milk on the table. It's really running just above the surface. I hit out at it, try to kill it with my towel. It cleverly avoids all my blows. Flies up in the air. I lash out wildly, without keeping my eye on the fly, I just brandish the towel. It snaps through the air. One of my blows hits home. Suddenly the fly is lying on the table in front of me. Beside the pool of milk. Just lying there. Right in front of me. I look at my victim with interest. At first it lies there apparently dead, on its back, legs at an angle. I blow at it. The little legs begin waving in the air. My puff has brought the breath of life back into it. It waves its legs some more, hesitantly turns over, gets on its legs again, begins crawling. It looks funny, left wing unfolded and sticking diagonally into the air. It can't fold the wing again. The other wing is dragging on the table. Damaged like that, it runs in a circle. Lost your sense of direction? Too bad, little fly, it's all over now, you can't bother me any more. Not you, you little horror. It tries to fly, gets into the milk again. It leaves a white, winding trail. I watch it for a long time until it begins to bore me, and I get tired of it. There you go then, sweetie. I flick the fly away with my forefinger.

I'm thirsty, I drink from the carton. I put my head back and let the milk run straight into my open mouth, swallow greedily. A thin trickle of liquid runs out of the corner of my mouth and then slowly down my throat. I put the empty carton down and wipe my mouth and my throat with the back of my hand. What little was left wasn't enough to quench my thirst. I look at the liquid on the table. A huge lake of milk made by that silly fly. Well, the fly paid for it. But I'm paying for it too! I'm thirsty, terribly thirsty. I turn my head to left and right, I know I'm alone in the room, but I still look around. I'd feel embarrassed to be watched and not know it. Maybe that guy has set up cameras all over the place? I'm the lab guinea pig in a new, perverted TV series. What does someone do when she's been abducted and shut up alone in a room? That's the idea. All secretly observed by a camera. A crazy TV show, with families sitting in front of the box at home wearing tracksuits, munching crisps and betting on what I'll do next. I bend over the table. If I purse up my lips I can get at the milk. A strand of hair comes loose, falls into it. I fish it out, push my hair back, hold it in place. Holding it with both hands, I begin sucking up the liquid with my pursed lips. There, that's quite something for you lot out there gawping at the box to watch! I slurp noisily, I stop for breath, and listen in case a noise somewhere gives away a camera running or a secret watcher after all. No, there's no one here. Well, dear audience, you really missed something! I suck up all the milk from the table. Done it! My lips feel furry with the sucking vibrations, as if I'd been playing the trumpet or blowing up balloons for hours.

What was that sound? A rumbling noise down below. Close to the stairs?

I gaze at the trapdoor. No creaking on the staircase, there's no one coming up. The door stays closed. Footsteps again, loud, clacking sounds, the footsteps move away and come back again.

Very cautiously, so as not to make any noise, I crawl on all fours over to the trapdoor. Lean my face slowly down to the crack until my eyebrows touch the wood.

There's someone there! All I can see is someone holding

83

a rabbit by its back legs, just the rabbit and the arm holding it. The rest is outside my field of vision. The rabbit is probably dead. No, suddenly it struggles and a short, violent twitch goes through its body several times. Then it hangs limp again. I was terribly frightened, but thank God I put my hand in front of my mouth just in time to keep from screaming. I don't want the man down there to notice me watching him.

Come on, you, take a step to the left, why don't you? I hear metal objects clinking and clattering. He seems to be looking for something in the cupboard by the front door.

He steps forward, and his body comes into view. Bright daylight falls on him from outside, emphasizing his striking features. On each side of his head there's a bald strip beginning at the temple and going down to his ear. A narrow strip, completely hairless, as if it has been shaved. Who on earth shaves his head in a pattern of stripes?

He turns, goes out of doors, there's nothing more to be heard. Silence. I look through the crack again, waiting. Nothing at all happens for a long time. After a while my knees hurt. I drag myself over to the bed and go on staring up at the ceiling. Why am I here? Why me? Why not the boss? He has the key to the safe, and anyway who'd care about old wobbly-jowls? But maybe this guy isn't after the money after all? He must have been watching me, to get into my apartment while I was out. Why did he take that picture? He can only have stolen it from my place. Who *is* this guy? Maybe he's been to our firm before. But there are lots of people going in and out of the place every day. Just his kind, with close-cropped or shaven hair and army surplus clothes. Most of them want to do some kind of shady business with the boss, something involving stolen cars. The staff don't officially know anything about that, but I'm not stupid. I keep my eyes open.

That weird haircut, two bald stripes down the sides of his head. I'd noticed them before. What kind of idiot shaves stripes like that into his hair? Could be they're birthmarks, or the result of an injury. Only a village idiot like Hans would go about looking like that...

My God – they're scars! An accident! No, no, this can't be true, this mustn't be true, I don't believe it!

The injuries left on Hans's head by the hay grab! Two bleeding wounds made by its gripping arms! Hans the village idiot who fancied little boys.

Hans, the last person to see Joachim alive. Presumed to have murdered him, not that anyone saw it. All I told the police was that Hans was the last person with him, nothing else. No, no, I never called him the murderer, at least not to the police. Of course everyone was sure he was guilty, who else would it have been? Me, his own sister? They took Hans straight away, everyone knew how aggressive he could be. He was the only possible suspect capable of such a cruel murder.

What became of him? They said he was crazy. Life in a mental hospital. He was a danger to the community. That's all I know. It was obvious, why talk about it? Dead is dead, and no one really liked Joachim. Even our stepmother was soon happy again, he'd just been a nuisance all round.

Can Hans have been released? A life sentence doesn't mean life any more. So he found me, well, that wasn't difficult. I haven't moved far, only to the next town. And then I cross his path in the local hire-car and used-car dealership. No, finding me wasn't difficult. He only had to keep his ears open in the village, most of my friends and relations still live there.

But why is he after me? Because of my evidence, obviously: I said Hans was the last person with him. And now I'm in trouble. He wants revenge. He's crazy.

I walk up and down the room. I don't want to have to think about what happened back then. I keep pressing my fists to my forehead. I was still a little kid, you don't think so much of what you're saying, what you're doing. There's a lot of things you do, and later you wish you hadn't. I'm sorry if he wasn't with Joachim that particular day after all. Hans was the one who'd be thought responsible. I only said out loud what everyone was thinking. Everyone in the village! Everyone!

Oh, bloody shit! How am I going to get out of this?

Years and years in the loony-bin, and who was responsible? Little Monika! She gave evidence to the court! At the time he kept on and on telling the court he was innocent, he hadn't done anything. He sat there and said it over and over again. They couldn't get anything else out of him. Just: 'It wasn't me'. No one believed him. And there was my evidence. The dead boy's sister wouldn't be telling lies.

If he was innocent, that would eat into him corrosively year after year. Deeper and deeper, and then he'd get around to hating the person who put an innocent boy behind bars. That's only logical. His hatred grows and grows, he discharges it the first time he sees that person again. All of a sudden, like that! He's making me writhe on the hook. Who knows what else he's planning to do to me? More than likely the beating I took was only the start.

I have to get out of here.

Maybe I can break the lock on the trapdoor? With the broken knife.

Where I felt metal resisting it last time, the knife meets a void. I can't believe it. The trapdoor isn't locked. Am I lucky! Now I mustn't make any mistakes. Go very carefully, make no noise. I pull at the door and it opens a crack. Pulling it up is easier than pushing it from below.

I wait for a moment. The stairs are empty, no one in sight on the ground floor. I keep perfectly still, hold my breath, listen. Nothing to be heard apart from a cricket chirping. A cool draught. That's all.

I pull the trapdoor further up with all my might, open it fully, lean it slowly and carefully against the wall without a sound. First my left foot on the first step, toes first, then slowly let the rest of the foot down until I'm standing on the entire sole. Step by step. A mouldy smell rises to my nostrils. After a few steps I bend down and peer at the large room beneath me under the open door. The door beyond the low brick partition is wide open. Hanging on the open door is a small body with its arms stretched. Like a baby's. The outline stands out clearly, the body itself is in shadow. I've opened my eyes wide, I stare at the body, go down the last few steps without taking my eyes off it. I start making my way towards the low brick wall and then along it, hardly daring to breathe. I'm taking smaller steps now. As I come closer, the body takes shape more clearly. No skin, just pale red, muscular flesh. Head and feet cut off. I notice how my throat is constricting more and more, I feel sick, just a step to the wall, propping myself on it with my hands, I vomit in a great gush against the wall. I let myself drop to the ground. A metre away from me there's a shallow tin pan. In it lie the rabbit's bloodstained skin and severed head.

It's all so disgusting. I have to get out of here, quick.

I scramble up, take another look at the skinned rabbit, turn and go over to the door opposite. I don't look left or right, just straight ahead. Over the threshold. The sun dazzles me for a moment, just disappearing behind the treetops. I cross the old wooden door. First cautiously, slowly, taking care to make no sound, then I move faster. Past the pond, through the undergrowth. I'm running. I ignore the thorny shoots catching in my blouse, tearing it. The path – left or right? Right or left? Which way did I get out of the car, was it to the right or the left of it? Damn it, my stupid sense of direction! Go on, think!

I can't concentrate, I don't know. Hell! Well, any direction, then. Right or left – heads or tails. Left! I run for a little way, but then my breath gives out. I get a stitch in my side, go down on my knees, gasping, I'm out of strength. All the same, I struggle on and on. It gets darker and darker. When I look at my shoes I see that I'm having difficulty lifting my feet from the ground. The path grows narrower, just a cart-track with two deep ruts. Grass in the middle. I switch to one of the ruts. It's full of broken tiles and stones, my steps sound louder and clearer than on firm ground. There are hardly any clouds in the sky, pale moonlight, black bushes beside the path.

The night is never entirely black. In the light of the moon, all the bushes look as if there were an animal or some other living creature hiding in them, or concealed behind them. I know that's nonsense. No one's out and about here at this time of night, and the only dangerous animals are in the zoo, not here. All the same, I'm frightened.

The cart-track gets even narrower, the central strip disappears, the road is nothing but a path leading into the forest now, winding its way up to a rise.

And now I realize that I turned the wrong way right at the start. The town is in the opposite direction. So silly of me – how could I be so stupid? Half-witted!

Frustrated and exhausted, I sit down on the path. My legs ache, my back hurts, and I'm cold. My mouth is dry. I'm thirsty. I sit there looking up at the moon. I feel like crying. Was that splashing I heard? If I keep quite still and concentrate on the bushes on the other side of the path, I seem to hear something splashing. A little stream? A spring of water? My exhaustion disappears. I jump up and force my way through the bushes, feeling the dusty ground. Nothing. I'll have to stay thirsty.

I go back through the bushes to the path. My eyes are used to the darkness now, so that's no trouble. Disappointed and tired, I sit down on the path again. I'm finished. I can't go on. I sit there with my legs drawn up and my arms around them, looking at the moon. The sky is clear and full of stars. Hundreds of sparkling points of light in the heavens. I don't know how long I look up, I just sit there. My eyes fill with tears, and I begin crying helplessly. I scream and sob, I keep hammering my fists on the ground like a lunatic. I'm weeping with fear and rage. As time goes on my tears dry up and I just sit there, powerless, looking up and thinking of nothing. I have to get up, I have to go on – OK, I mean go back – before I actually give up the ghost. I have to go back to the house and try to find the right way from there. There's no other option. Either I die of thirst or I go back to my point of departure and try again, but in the other direction. With difficulty, I get to my feet. There are a few berries on a bush right beside me. They look like little black globules in the moonlight. I pick a handful, not many. Quickly put four or five in my mouth at once. The flavour is slightly sweet, fruity. The berries are full of seeds. I swallow. They have a bitter aftertaste. I spit. Now my mouth feels even drier and my tongue more coated than before. I throw the rest of the berries away.

If the bushes looked rather like dangerous animals earlier, now they seem to be human beings. I feel as if they're eyeing me, sitting up above me as if they were in the front of the circle at the theatre. They're staring at me. They sit there in old-fashioned garments. Some are staring at me, holding opera glasses up to their eyes, others are standing, nodding their heads, with glasses of champagne in their hands. I'm starting to have hallucinations, what with my thirst and my exhaustion. But I can see quite clearly how one of the theatre-goers leans far out over the front of the circle as I pass. I'm afraid. He's leaning too far over, he'll fall head first. He touches me, I can feel the breath of some of the spectators. They're spurring me on. Their calls grow louder, most of them are calling out encouraging remarks, they sound cheerful and emotional. The rows fill up more and more, there's pushing and shoving. The background sound grows louder. Glasses clink. First the restless spectators start whispering and murmuring, then they're calling out, the sound rises to shouting. I put my hands over my ears, the noise is almost unbearable. My heart is racing.

Go on. I'm gasping for breath. On and on, through the dense undergrowth. I see lights to my right, soon I'll reach the place where the path branches and leads to the mill.

Now they're lining my way, I have to push through the

crowd. I see their heated faces, red cheeks, gleaming eyes, I see them laughing with their mouths wide open. They crowd towards me. Their hands reach out for me, touch my arms, my shoulders. I can feel the warmth of their bodies standing close, side by side. The air smells used, acrid. I see the house. The audience is crowded together in a semi-circle now. They give way before me and leave the path free. Now I'm standing on the edge of the stage, the spectators have closed in around me again. I look around; the stage shows a ruinous old mill, light coming through little windows. The door is slightly open. I look back at the audience. Not a sound now, the crowd stands still. The human wall moves slowly, soundlessly towards me. I run to the door of the mill. The metal door sticks, won't open any wider, I have to force myself through it.

I go through the door, the stage swivels and now I'm in a different set of scenery. Lamps hang from the wall on long nails near the low brick wall. They cast beams of light on the stone floor. My glance wanders from one beam of light to another. Beyond the last one, someone is standing in front of a closed door in the dim light. I go up to him. Now he seems to notice me and turns around. He has a knife with a curved blade in one hand, a tubular reddish-grey shape in the other. He lets it go, it lands on the floor with a squelch.

Dark, mushy stuff comes out, forms a little lake that spreads, fills the cracks in the stones. Runs on, slowly making its way to the next stone.

I look up. There's a gutted body dangling there, with a thin trickle of blood running down. The hand holding the knife hangs limp and powerless.

He's a murderer, he murdered him. Slaughtered and gutted him like an animal. I was right, he did it, he murdered him.

My God, what's the matter with her? Hair in a mess, face bright red, swollen and scratched. Everything about her filthy. She must have run through the forest. I've been searching it for her, she wasn't there. I drove the Fiesta back to the road, very slowly. Stopped again and again, searched the forest to right and left. No sign of her. I'd started reconciling myself to the idea that she'd got away. How else was I to look for her? Just running around the forest is no use, at least not on your own. She could have been anywhere. I'd never expected to see her again so soon. It was plain stupid of me to carry the crockery downstairs and then forget to go back and bolt the trapdoor. Seems to run in the family. Father once forgot to bolt it too. Looks like we always make the same mistake in our family. Mother came back as well. I've been lucky.

But there's something not quite right about her. Is she drunk? Standing there with her legs apart, but all the same she's staggering around, can hardly stay upright. Looks like she'd lose her balance and fall over. Good heavens, girl, pull yourself together!

Her eyes are wide, black and gleaming, her glance is crazy. She stretches her whole arm out and points her fore-finger at me. Instinctively I look at the finger, it wavers back and forth. Now she opens her mouth – but she can't get a word out. I stand there too, gaping at her. The way she stands with her mouth open reminds me of a toad. Girl, if you just keep on breathing in the whole time like that you'll burst. Like a toad with a burning cigarette in its mouth. Bang, there it goes, blown to a thousand fragments.

She starts muttering something to herself. First quietly, I can't understand what she's saying, I can only hear the mur-muring and I see her moving her lips. Then it gets louder. My God, what's she up to? Stupid as shit, first running off, then coming back again. And now she stands there talking utter nonsense. She's lost her marbles. All I can make out is, 'You bastard!' and 'You murdered my brother!' Her voice gets louder and louder until she shouts, 'By rights I ought to give your name to the police.' The way she says that! 'I doubted myself, I thought it was my own fault.' She might be playing a part on stage in a theatre. 'But it was you who did it, you, you!' It sounds so artificial, all put on. 'And me with a guilty conscience for years, all because of you, you useless creature.'

Then she collapses entirely. Crying, screaming, sobbing. She's gone right off her head.

'Shut up, will you, or you'll be sorry!'

She doesn't stop, goes on shouting at me, screeching the same thing over and over again like crazy. 'You bastard!' She takes off, runs towards me. Her body is shaking, she swings her arm back. What's her idea? Is she out of her mind? She's beside herself.

She's closed her eyes.

She runs straight into my fist.

I lie there on my stomach, the cold cement floor under me. A musty cellar smell. I feel awful. My arms and legs are scratched. My grazes are burning. My head aches. He dragged me down to the cellar by my hair. Every root of it hurts. My mouth is dry, my tongue feels thick and swollen, glutinous saliva sticking my mouth up. I need something to drink. With difficulty, I haul myself up, look around. A paraffin lamp hangs from the hook beside the iron door, bringing a little light into the dark room.

I shake the door handle, but the door won't open. Maybe there's another way out? I take the lamp off the hook and look around. I'm in a long cellar – this room and two others, each opening off the one before it. In the last room there's an old iron bedstead. That's all. No other way out, no window. I sit on the bed and stare ahead of me. This time he didn't undress me, put me to bed and cover me up. He's leaving you here to die, I think. That bastard is leaving you here to die! The thought makes me so furious that I jump up, take the lamp and go over to the iron door.

I hammer on the door with my fist. Until the knuckles hurt. Then I go on hitting it with the palm of my hand. 'You bastard, let me out of here! I want to get out of here! Do you hear me? Open this door!'

I start crying, snot and tears running over my face. I let myself drop to the floor by the door, sit on the cement and go on crying. I'm crying with rage, I'm crying with pain. These last few days I have tried to pull myself together, tried not to lose control, and now it all comes spilling out of me. I can't stop crying.

But only a few minutes later I calm down. Suddenly my mind is curiously clear. How can I get out of here? He wanted the key. That's how it all began. He wanted money, the key to the safe. That's it, I must use that as bait. With money he'll forget the past, forget that he wants his revenge on me. With his sparrow-sized brain, I'm surprised he can even remember that far back.

Right, then, try your luck. There must still be a chance

for me. Maybe my last chance.

How to go about it? So far I've just been acting – or rather reacting – out of my gut feelings. And every time I land deeper in the shit. I need a plan, a strategy. Sounds good, only how do I do it?

Point One: he mustn't know that I know who he is. So no talking about the past, nothing about Joachim.

Point Two: this guy is aggressive, whatever I do I must avoid provoking any more violence from him.

Point Three: he always had problems with women. He's totally inhibited, and then all that time in jail or the loony-bin, you're bound to get inhibited in there. So what to do? Make up to him, exploit his insecurity with women!

I wipe the tears from my face with the back of my hand and stand up.

'Hello!' I hesitantly tap my finger against the door. Be nice to him, be friendly. I wait, put my ear to the door – nothing happens. Must have said it too quietly, he could be upstairs, who knows where? I knock on the door with my fist. 'Hello there! Open the door, please!'

Nothing stirs. I was probably too quiet again, he's sure to be out there. Now I hammer on the door with both fists. 'Hello! Open up! You arsehole, if you don't open up right now I'll…!' I kick it. Oh, don't go on like that. You stupid girl, you mustn't provoke him. You'll do just the opposite of what you're planning.

So try something new. Knock on that door in a more restrained way, wait, listen. I'm not sure, but I think I hear footsteps.

I knock on the door again. 'Hello, Hans, I'd like to get out of here. I know you want the key to the safe where I work. I know how we can get hold of it. I can help you, but only if you let me out. I'm no use at all to you in here, none at all. There's money in my boss's safe, a lot of money. I know how we can get the key. You won't get your hands on it without me, you need me! We can work together.'

Not a sound. 'Hello, did you understand what I said? We can work together. I'll help you. Let me out of here and I'll help you.' Silence. Was I wrong about the footsteps?

Suddenly I have a feeling of being stared at from all sides. I turn very quickly. Nothing. Just this long dark room. I want to get out of here! My mouth is dry, my jaws hurt. My heart is beating incredibly fast.

I turn back to the door, shake the handle. Tug it and pull it. Hold it firmly with both hands, push it down with all my might. Click. The door opens. It wasn't locked at all, just stuck. I was too stupid to try opening it.

I begin laughing hysterically. My voice sounds strange

to me, but after a little while I calm down again. I'm calm now. Perfectly calm.

I leave the cellar, go up the stairs. On my right the closed door, nothing to be seen of the dead rabbit now. But the floor under the place where it was dangling is covered by something dark and gleaming. My eyes wander over the rest of the room, which is a little lower than this part, and has nothing interesting about it except for old machinery and wooden things. My heart starts beating hard again. I can hear it pulsating in my ears. I go over to the stairs. The trapdoor is above me. I was imprisoned up there for several days. It's dark, which is a relief to my eyes; bright light hurts them.

There's no one in the house apart from me. It's eerie, there's a strange, ominous feeling about the mill. As if it were alive. As if pairs of eyes were watching me from every nook and cranny. I go on to the iron front door. As before, it's just a crack open. I force myself through the gap; it's almost entirely dark outside. Only a flickering light coming through from the side of the house is cast on the surrounding bushes. It all looks unreal, like before. I go along the wall of the house in the direction of the light. Peer around the corner of the building, through the metal remains of an old millwheel.

He's standing in front of a camp fire, his long shadow

dances in front of me. Above the fire, on a spit, there's a long-ish piece of meat. He's holding a bottle in one hand and slowly turning the spit with the other. The smell of the camp fire lies over everything.

I can't shake off the sense of being watched. I look around, can't see anyone. Oh, pull yourself together. You'll go crazy this way. This is real. The guy is grilling something on a spit, that's all. Now then, go over there, eat something, soft-soap him into helping you, and then the first chance you get you can finally disappear. It'd be funny if you couldn't manage that. It's just that I'll never get away from here on my own.

I stop. I'm standing at an angle behind him, trying not to stare at the fire. Its light dazzles me. I look at the spit he's just taking off the fire. The meat looks rather charred and has a slightly sweetish smell. I still have that dry feeling in my mouth. It won't go away, however much I swallow. Well, here we both are. Right, I'll take the first step.

I don't need to turn round. I can hear her coming out of the mill and moving towards me.

She stops, stands at an angle behind me. She waits, then starts talking to me.

'What are you doing?'

She seems to have come to her senses again. Speaks normally.

'Barbecuing meat, you can see that.'

She comes a step closer, I turn to her, the spit with the rabbit on it in one hand, vodka bottle in the other. I see her face in the flickering light of the camp fire. She still looks confused and odd. Is it the fire? Her face is very flushed. Now she comes quite close to me. Only inches away. I think I can feel her breath.

She stares at me. Eyes wide open, pupils incredibly big and black. Almost nothing of the irises of her eyes shows. She talks to me, quietly, fast. Very fast! Very quietly. All I can make out are scraps of words: 'Wanted...say...know where the key...take me back...never get the key without me... money...'

She keeps rambling on. There's no stopping her. But I can only make out bits and pieces. 'Child...murderer... rabbit...eyes everywhere...dead.'

She's completely round the bend, that's what goes through my head, better not let her see I know it. Who knows what she might do? She's as crazy as they come! I ought not to have locked her in, that sends a lot of people round the twist. They can't cope with it. It was the same in jail. Someone was always going off his head.

He stands there in front of me with the spit in his hand. All I can hear is the thudding and ringing in my ears. I look at the spit, don't want to but can't look away. I see arms in the flickering light. I see arms and legs!

I rush forward in panic, right up to the fire, reach with both hands for one of the burning pieces of wood.

I see the guy staring at me in surprise. Eyes wide, mouth open. He drops the bottle and the spit, raises both arms, holds them in front of his face to protect it. I keep bringing the piece of wood down on his head. Embers everywhere, sparks leaping in all directions. Burning bits of wood eat little circles in his short hair. Wisps of smoke rise. There's a smell of burnt hair. He lowers his arms and stares at me. I stand in front of him, the piece of wood still in my hands. I see his horrified glance; I look at my hands. Blackened, blackened all over. And now I feel the pain. My hands won't let go of the wood. That wall of spectators, they're all around me again. Coming closer without a sound. The spectators stand close together round the fire, their faces grave.

She collapsed beside the fire, the piece of wood still in her hands. My God. She's in shock. And no wonder; her hands look charred, they're stuck to the burning wood. Must get it off, she has to plunge those hands into cold water. I learnt that on my paramedic course in the army. Our instructor held a container of peas in front of our noses, shook it vigorously back and forth and blathered on – something about molecular movement that had to be halted with plenty of cold water. OK then, water! The bucket is standing by the stairs. I fetch it, run to the water butt and fill it with cold water.

I come back with the full bucket. She's kneeling by the fire, raising and lowering the thing that's a combination of her arms and the piece of wood, babbling nonsense. She's off her rocker. What have I let myself in for? She's going to freak out again any moment. Vodka! She needs alcohol to deaden the pain and numb her, and to get the charred bits off her hands. Right, one thing at a time. First, to stop the burning. I tip the water over her hands – there's hissing and smoke. She doesn't even notice, just crouches there babbling on. I go carefully all the same, she's violent. Now the vodka. I hold my bottle to her lips. She drinks in big, greedy gulps.

I don't know if it's the shock, the vodka or whether she's cracked up completely now. She smiles, sits there grinning madly to herself while I get the charred wood off her hands with the help of the alcohol. Or rather I get the wood and the skin off her hands. Not a pretty sight. Like skinning the rabbit. At least the rabbit was dead.

I quickly get the first-aid box out of the car. Let's hope the silly cow stays sitting there and doesn't start on anything else, but drunk as she is she can't move from the spot. There's even a packet of dressings for burns in the first-aid box, who'd have thought it? Right, cover the burn dressing with cotton wool as padding, I get that from the mill, then another layer of ordinary bandage. Now she's wearing thick white boxing gloves. They suit her, and I feel safer.

The patient, now entirely naked, is carefully moved to the operating table. The respiratory tube, blood pressure monitor and venous cannulas are all checked by the anaesthetist. Legs and arms are strapped to the operating table. The metal frame to secure the green operating cloth is screwed down. The cloth is stretched over the frame level with the patient's neck. Only the body is now in the surgeon's field of vision.

A swab is inserted into a pair of forceps. The stomach area is wiped down three times with the swab, which is soaked in a solution of alcohol. The brownish-red liquid forms a little reflecting puddle in the navel. It runs over the stomach and drips off both sides of the body on to the operating table.

Two smooth parallel lines on the skin, coloured dark by the disinfectant, are all that can now be seen of the cleansed stomach wound.

My head hurts horribly. The pain's at the front, in my forehead, moving to both sides. The pressure on my temples feels as if my whole skull is jammed in a vice with someone slowly tightening it. Every time my eyes move, even if they're closed, the thudding starts up. My whole skull is ringing with the sound. I feel sick.

My tongue is sticking to my gums. I can get it loose only with difficulty by clicking it. I still feel thirsty. Terribly thirsty. I move my tongue around in my mouth. At first just poking cautiously, my mouth gets a little moister, then I move it back and forth between my cheeks and my jaws a couple of times. A dull, bitter taste spreads through my mouth. Then there's a sour one as my gorge rises. I feel so sick.

My hands are pulsating, no, going wild. My fingers will hardly move, as if they were frozen. They're strangely heavy. They're inside something, it feels like gloves. What's going on? I must open my eyes. Open them! I know this headache will kill me, but I have to know what's the matter with my hands. Was I drunk yesterday? I can't remember anything about it. It's all a blackout.

I open my eyes. The same wooden ceiling, I'm back in bed in the mill. Covered up again. What's the matter with my hands? They're lying on the quilt, thickly bandaged.

I sit up and stare at them. Huge white Christmas tree baubles.

Now that I'm sitting upright in bed the throbbing in my hands gets worse. They feel terribly hot. The pulsating and the heat feel worse every second. I must get this bandaging off, I can't stand the heat.

Damn it, it won't come off. I get the end of the sticking plaster between my teeth. I begin pulling the bandaging off my right hand. Good heavens, how many layers of stuff are there? The sticking plaster clings to my lips. Fibres of bandage get stuck in my teeth. At last I've unwrapped the bandage, strip by strip. Now for the cotton wool. I try shaking it off, every movement of my hand hurts horribly. I pull the rest off with my teeth. The cotton wool sticks to them;

I spit and blow it out. Another layer of bandaging. The more bandaging and cotton wool I get off, the stronger it smells of burning. The taste spreads right through my mouth like something charred. The bandaging has more and more black marks and stripes as I get it off. The last layers are soaked in something reddish-brown. I look at my hand. I feel sick again. It's not my hand any more, it's a lump of charred, stinking flesh.

I'm not back at the house yet when I hear her screaming and shouting. She screams like a wild animal. No wonder, the effect of the alcohol has worn off and she's in pain. I run the last of the way to the house. Better get in there fast before she goes stark raving mad. She's beside herself; the silly cow will end up falling downstairs and breaking her neck. Then I really will be in the shit! I almost slip on the wooden door lying on the ground, just stop myself falling over in time. Through the metal door, over to the staircase.

Her screaming is almost unbearable inside the house. I left the trapdoor open on purpose; she can't get down the steps with those hands anyway. The unwrapped end of the bandage is hanging through the hatch. It almost reaches the low brick wall across the room. Standing on the first step of the stairs, I look up.

She's standing right above me. One leg on the first step. Both arms slightly spread, forearms raised, her left hand is still completely covered with white bandaging. She's almost unwrapped the bandages on the right hand, there's only a little muslin still sticking to it.

I try to calm her down, climbing the stairs slowly, step by step. I talk to her soothingly all the time. I don't want her freaking out again and maybe jumping through the hatch. Soothing them always works with my rabbits, it takes their fear away. She seems to be calming down, too. She looks at me. White as a sheet. I can see she's in a bad way, just by looking at her. Her eyes are normal again, the pupils aren't dilated like they were yesterday. She's swaying. Hell, I hope she doesn't fall. If she falls now she'll land on me, and then both of us will crash to the stone floor.

'Stop there! I'm coming up, I'll help you. I've got something for the pain. Go back and lie down on the bed. I'll help you!'

She starts trembling, her body shakes, she's swaying more and more.

Get up there fast now, or she'll fall. Two steps at a time, I'm making my way up with arms and legs at the same time.

I ram my head into her stomach and she falls backwards – can't break her fall with her arms.

I'm half-lying on her, my head on her lower body. She's turning her head back and forth, whimpering.

'It hurts. Hurts badly. I can't stand it any more. Help me! I can't stand it any more!'

I stand up, take her under the arms and drag her over to the bed. I heave her up on the mattress like a sack of flour. Instead of doing anything to help, she just wails quietly to herself, makes herself heavier by stretching out.

I tip the contents of my plastic bag out on the bed. Needles, syringe, the stuff itself, and some citric acid. It cost a packet. She lies there, writhing about, whining and whimpering to herself. I can't just let her lie here and leave her to die.

'Watch out, you'll have everything on the floor!'

'Help me! It hurts so much!'

I unpack the syringe and the needle, open the little bag with the stuff in it. A small amount of the white powder in a spoon. There, let's hope that's enough. Too little will do no good, too much and she'll die. A few drops of citric acid on it. Mix it up with a few drops of water from the bottle, cigarette lighter underneath the spoon, bring it all to the boil. A small piece of muslin to make it easier to draw up.

A single-use syringe, put the needle in, remove the plastic cap. Done it.

'Keep still!'

I fasten the belt around her upper arm. She twists and turns, hits out. I tighten the belt, the veins on her forearm stand out slightly.

'There, keep still now.'

The skin in the crook of her elbow tenses as the needle goes in. She tries to pull her arm away but I hold it firmly, press the plunger down in the syringe. The liquid disappears into her body.

Almost at once her head stops turning this way and that, her tightly closed eyes relax, so do the muscles of her face. She's breathing deeply and slowly. Her mouth opens, a smile appears, she begins to moan. She looks quite peaceful now.

After a minute she closes her mouth and falls asleep. There's only a quiet murmuring to be heard.

Bloody hell! Now I have a seriously ill woman on my hands. I ought to have planned this whole thing better. I'm so in the shit.

I have to dress her hands again or she'll cap it all by getting blood poisoning. Let's hope I didn't forget anything in my hurry. I unwrap the old dressing layer by layer – it sticks to the skin, or rather to what's left of it. I moisten the dressing, then it comes off better. Little Brother Vodka comes in useful again. First a gulp from the bottle, then clean the wounds with the soaked compress. What you've once learnt you don't forget. New dressing and bandage, there we are.

She lies there sleeping peacefully.

I dream of the meadow again. I turn and run away, with my dress blowing in the wind and my plaits dancing. The meadow is full of dandelions. A sea of green flecked with yellow. I run on. I come to a little stream, jump over it. The grass hasn't been mown on the other side. It gets taller and taller. Grasses and wild flowers come up to my waist. Butterflies are fluttering about, I put out my hand and a little blue butterfly settles on it. I can feel it licking salt off my skin with its proboscis. I put my face down very close to it, puff at it. It spreads its wings and flies away. I watch it go. The sun's shining into my face, the light is so bright that I have to put my hand up to shield my eyes. I feel incredibly light and happy. I want to go on, on and on, running and jumping until I'm out of breath. Hands on my bare knees, I breathe deeply in and out. The scent of the freshly mown meadow is in my nostrils. I'd like to stay in the lovely meadow. I'd like to stay here.

The meadow turns, and I'm back standing on the stage again. But it's not a real stage, I'm tiny, terribly tiny. A hand is reaching for me. Reaching down into the set from above, as if it were a box. I run into a corner and try to hide, crouch down, make myself even smaller. No, I don't want this, no! Stop lifting me out of here. The hand closes around me as if I were a little bird. I want to stay here. Let go, no!

I see the wooden ceiling, the stupid wooden ceiling. I've woken up so often to see that filthy wooden ceiling. I try to push the quilt back. Stupid quilt. My hands are thickly bandaged and the throbbing in them is starting again. I can't think of anything else. The pain goes all along my arms. Bloody hell, I want it to stop! I want to get out of here.

That guy is sitting on the bed beside me. Grinning. My God, what a shock. I quickly look back at the quilt, don't want to talk to this grinning character. What does the oaf want? He's supposed to be helping me.

I feel awful. Suddenly there's a terrible pressure in my stomach. Everything coming together there. I have this big lump in my throat, I don't want to bring it up.

'I feel sick!' And it all comes up and gushes out of me in a torrent. I throw up over everything, the bed, the guy, everything. Again and again, I retch, I feel as if my stomach's turning upside down. Everything hurts. I have a stitch in both sides. I feel as if my stomach itself were coming up, as if my guts were tearing loose, and I can't stop spewing it out until my body's entirely empty. I retch again and again, although there's nothing left to bring up.

Exhausted, I drop back on the pillow. I'm wet with cold sweat. My stomach won't stop contracting. It's several minutes before it slowly calms down.

Only the eyes in the faces of the operating team show, everything else is covered by their face masks and caps. The surgeon wears horn-rimmed glasses. Their thick lenses make his eyes look unnaturally large. Hands protected by sterile single-use gloves, the surgeon introduces his forefinger and middle finger into the wounds of the stomach cavity. Concentrating entirely on his sense of touch. He isn't even looking at the patient, he's looking straight ahead, impassively, at the operating theatre. 'The lower stab wound didn't penetrate the peritoneum, you can stitch that afterwards, here. We only have to work on the upper wound.'

Without looking at his assistant, who is standing opposite him at the operating table, the surgeon makes these remarks to him in an undertone. He asks for a scalpel. Extends the wound by about two centimetres up and two centimetres down. The young doctor opposite him watches every move closely, nodding vigorously.

The sharp scalpel moves lightly over the skin, but an incision immediately appears. Light red blood comes out in three or four places, sometimes in a thin jet. It is quickly staunched with compresses, and the sites of the bleeding are cauterized with an electric burner. Little clouds of smoke rise, and there's a smell of burning in the nostrils of the team standing around the patient. The bleeding stops.

'There's food on the table. Your clothes are at the end of the bed. They're still wet, I washed them as best I could.'

He's bandaged my hands again, washed my clothes, prepared a meal and laid the table. What *does* he want me for? He's attacked me, beaten me up, brought me here and kept me prisoner in this place. Is he a normal criminal? It makes no sense. It wasn't coincidence. He's carrying out a plan. He must have planned to abduct me. Is he some kind of pervert? A pervert who kidnaps women, tortures them and keeps them prisoner? How did he get hold of that photo? He must have been in my apartment. But why? Obviously he's been spying on me. It all fits Hans. Hans wanting to get his revenge. He was after me, not the money. The attack was just for show, the real idea, the point of the whole thing, was abducting me! The photo backs that up, why else the photo? The photo. That's the key to the whole thing. I must get it out of him. But how?

By talking to him, building up a link with him. The stronger the link between us, the harder it will be for him to kill me, just get me out of the way. Sort of like the Stockholm syndrome in reverse. There was an article about that in the newspaper. But does he simply want to do away with me? He's tended my hands, washed my things, cooked for me. Maybe he wants both revenge *and* the money?

For now I'm dependent on him. I can't even dress or feed myself, I can't go to the loo by myself. I hate this. I can't do anything on my own, anything at all, I even have to ask him to put my knickers on me. I'm absolutely dependent on this guy. Does he like that, does it turn him on? I could have got away more than once. Not now, though, I can't even get down that steep staircase without his help. I can't hold on to anything with my hands in this state. I've got myself into one hell of a mess. I ought to be terribly afraid. But I'm not. I'm perfectly calm, it's as if it is nothing to do with me. As if I am sitting inside a bubble or a glass ball. I can see and hear everything, but nothing gets through to me. I'm composed, which is really odd. I ought to be screaming, raging, crying, defending myself. But I'm just calmly observing things. Sitting behind the glass wall inside me, separated from myself. Absolutely crazy. Well, it makes no difference if he's Hans or some other weirdo, I have to get him on my side. I don't stand a chance unless I get him on my side. My only chance. Oh God, help me!

The first thing I must do is get dressed, and then we'll see. I'll have to ask him to help. 'Can you help me get dressed, please?'

He nods. This is terribly embarrassing for me. He helps me into my clothes. He doesn't seem to mind doing that – if anything the opposite.

'Thank you.'

He goes over to the table and sits down. I stand where I am in the room, undecided.

'Hungry? Come and have something to eat.'

With an inviting wave of his hand he beckons me over. I go towards him, sit down. He smiles at me. I try a smile myself, stretching the corners of my mouth rather awkwardly.

I have to be fed like a toddler. Forkful after forkful, now and then a sip of water to wash it down.

'Have some more?'

'No, I've had enough.'

'Right, then I'll take the dishes down to the sink.'

He stands up and begins clearing the table. I don't want to be left alone again, I just don't want it. All at once I'm scared of that, scared of being alone, afraid of my dreams.

'Can you stay here?'

He doesn't say anything, but he sits down again. So there we sit in silence. Each of us looking at the table top. After a while I hear myself speaking to him, very quietly. 'I don't want to be alone.'

He doesn't say a word. Sits there in silence. I just go on talking, talking about anything. Talking so he'll stay and I won't be alone.

'Is this house yours?'

'Why do you want to know?'

'Only wondering.'

A pause. Shit, that was the wrong question.

'What's your name?'

'You can call me whatever you like.'

'But you must have a name! How about Hans? I'll call you Hans.'

'It's as good as any other name.'

'Do you like Hans? Is it all right if I call you that?'

'Go ahead, if you want to.'

He sits there and doesn't say any more. Just stares at his

hands. I sit there and don't say any more either. Damn it, this isn't working, I can't think of anything to say to him, can't have a reasonable conversation with him. There's a wall between us. Joachim, dead Joachim? All I know is that if I'm left alone again I'll go crazy. I don't want to be alone, can't be alone. Everything revolves around that one idea: I don't want to be alone.

He stands up. Takes the tray. I stand up too, get in his way.

'I know where the key is. I can help you get the money, Hans.'

He stops in surprise, looks at me. For the first time he looks me straight in the eye. It tumbles out of me. I just go on talking.

'I can help you, and then you'll let me go, OK?'

He looks at me suspiciously, tries to get past me with the tray. I step the wrong way, collide with the tray. Everything falls to the floor with a clatter.

'Sorry.'

He looks at me, pushes a strand of hair out of my face with his hand. Almost tenderly. Holds my head between his big hands. I close my eyes. He kisses me right on the mouth. Then he picks the broken china up from the floor, takes the tray and goes. I'm just left standing there in the middle of the room.

*

I wake up, and my hands are throbbing like crazy. Going wild. I'm beginning to go wild myself, I'm screaming. Turning this way and that in the bed.

'Hans, help me. I can't stand this! Give me another injection! Help me! Oh, please help me!'

A loud crashing and rumbling. He runs up the stairs, gets the plastic bag and shakes out the contents on the bed beside me. What's he doing? Making a mixture of powder of some kind, water, lemon juice. Heats it all up in a spoon over his cigarette lighter. Draws it up into the syringe.

'Here we go. This won't hurt.'

He knows how to give an injection, I have to admit that. He sits on the bed beside me. Takes me in his arms, holds me tight.

My toes and fingertips go hot, gradually my arms and feet warm up too. The heat races through my body, up to my breast, gathers in my head. I'm burning! I'm surprised, it doesn't hurt, I'm not in pain, on the contrary, it's a pleasant feeling. Like a wave building up in the water and then running in to shore faster and faster until it breaks. The warmth turns to a soft sensation, everything feels lighter, inside and outside.

I feel as if I could take off from the ground, rise and hover in the air, overcome gravity. I've closed my eyes tightly, but everything is still bright, almost glaringly bright. All the same, it's nice. Everything is incredibly bright and colourful. Red light around the rim, then brighter and darker colours alternating, converging on the middle of the picture in a semi-circle. In the middle there's a deep blue.

The blue gets lighter, washes itself out, I see a stage.

A tree in the middle of the big stage, a willow tree made of papier mâché, with coloured leaves. Mist slowly rises. There are two people on the stage. One, the smaller one, is lying down. The other, an adult, is standing beside the first.

What is this, a play, an opera? The actor who is standing purses his lips, opens his mouth wide, shows his teeth. It's all done very slowly. I wait for a sound, but no sound comes out. I can see that the actor is singing. But there's not a note to be heard. No, that's not quite right, I do hear a sound. Very quiet at first, then rising, growing stronger and stronger, like whimpering from the orchestra pit. The sound swells, grows louder, dies away, only to rise again. I'm sitting in the front row of the stalls, right behind the orchestra pit. I lean forward, peer over the bar in front of the seats. All the chairs in the pit are empty. There's only one musician there in his tailcoat, sitting to one side of the conductor's rostrum. He's moving the bow of a violin over the blunt edge of a huge handsaw. The saw is jammed between his knees, his free hand holds the top of it, he is pressing it down hard so that the blade curves slightly. His expression is grave, almost rapt.

I lean back again, looking expectantly at the stage. The smaller character, the one lying down, is clothed in a sheet, stomach sprayed with bright red paint. One ear is bright red as well. Now this other actor also begins to sing, but without a sound. I can tell from the movement of the lips, the singer's gestures show what an effort he is making. Lying there, he keeps pointing to his stomach with one hand, and with the other to the standing actor.

The standing actor raises both arms, fending everything off with exaggerated gestures and wide open eyes. Those faces remind me of the actors' pottery masks of classical antiquity that were once painted in bright colours. I saw some in the showcases of the Municipal Museum. The lighting changes; now the larger actor looks like an American Indian in warpaint. Marks like stripes run down both sides of his skull.

The curtain falls. In the pit, the musician puts down his bow and the saw, takes a red banana out of his jacket pocket, starts thoughtfully peeling it. And as he looks up at me he slowly eats the banana. He glances at the time, quickly puts the banana peel down, picks up his instrument and the bow, and begins playing that dreadful, monotonous melody again.

The curtain rises. The same set as before, but this time the musical accompaniment breaks off in the middle of the scene. The musician has gone to sleep; only the falling curtain wakes him. He comes to with a start and jumps up. He inspects his musical instrument closely, then sits down again. The actors come on stage and bow deeply.

My loud clapping re-echoes, all by itself. I look around. I am the only spectator. I lean over the bar in front of me and look down into the orchestra pit. The musician bows very low to me. He is holding the violin bow in one hand and the saw in the other. He takes both saw and bow in his left hand and begins waving his other hand.

Mist gathers on the floor of the stage, flows slowly over the edge of the platform and down into the orchestra pit. Envelops the musician, swallows him up. Everything turns blue, but with a reddish tinge at the edges, and slowly changes to a bright red.

I feel sick.

I open my eyes, see the wooden ceiling above the bed.

I'm lying in the Fiesta in a sleeping bag. The side window is open and I breathe in the forest smells. I waited until she'd gone to sleep. Only then did I leave the mill and go down the path beside the pond to my car. I slept here the last two nights, and there was no one to notice. No one's waiting for me. I like to sleep with a window open. That was the worst part of jail. Having to share a cell with four others. The air in the cells was stale and musty. The neon lighting had red dimmers fitted to turn down the glaring tubes. You get woken up at six in the morning. The clatter of the drop-down hatch for your food. Noise everywhere all of a sudden. If you make out you're still asleep the prison officers come in, clash their keys against the metal bedstead and pull the covers off. Then you get up and wait for breakfast. Half a litre of dishwater, you can't call that thin brew coffee, rye bread, jam. Honey and nut spread only once every two weeks. If one of the officers didn't like you he'd spill the hot coffee over your fingers or pour it out beside the mug instead of in it. You couldn't defend yourself or complain. If you did complain all the same, there'd be a beating after eight when you were locked into the cells and 'proper penal correction' began. You want to keep out of that, keep your mouth shut, look for ways of working your way up the hierarchy. So that you're the one who spills coffee over other people's fingers, the one who hands out physical punishment or extra work. The one who keeps his mouth shut and plays it by the book. Working your way up.

The ones who fucked little kids never work their way up, they stay at the bottom of the heap. There always has to be someone you can kick. I'd learnt how to keep my mouth shut from Father. Knew it was best to be like the three monkeys: see no evil, hear no evil, speak no evil.

I could sleep down in the bunker, but I don't want to; I'm not at ease there. I'd rather sleep here in the car. The bunker was Father's place. I always feel as if he's watching me when I'm down there. I can't get to sleep in the bunker, it's like sleeping in jail – the air is stale and it's dark. Feeling you're not free to move is the worst of it. That's why I put her up in Mother's room. It's healthier there and more comfortable.

She's like Mother; she reminds me of Mother. *She* can't bear to be on her own either. Like Mother, she begged me not to leave her alone. Just like Mother.

Mother used to cling to Father too. Begged him not to leave her alone. Not to lock her up in the mill again. He beat her and pushed her away from him. Sitting down in my hiding place, I heard her screams.

I heard them quarrelling again, I heard him hitting her again. I heard her pleading. But Father went away and left her alone.

And then Mother went away herself. Later, I found out that she'd hanged herself in the mill because she couldn't bear it any longer. After three days of being locked in, she hanged herself.

I'm not such a bastard as he was. I don't want to be that kind of an arsehole. I'll stay here, I won't leave her alone. She needs me, like Mother needed me when Father beat her, and like she needed me when Father had locked her into the mill.

The scalpel slides into tissue again. Places where new bleeding appears are cauterized at once. Fatty tissue spills out, the surgeon goes on and on, working his way into the depths. Carefully feeling about with his gloved hands, going far into the abdominal cavity.

'Right, everyone. Now we make an incision in the musculature, then after the peritoneum we get to work on the intestine.' The surgeon smiles. Raises his head, looks briefly at his young colleague. The operating mask hides his face, which still shows no expression.

Broad silvery metal retractors are set in place. The assistant grasps their handles and hold the abdominal wall open.

Shiny grey intestine fills the stomach cavity. The surgeon's whitish, gleaming, rubber-gloved hands go in among the slippery, elastic intestinal loops. Feel the internal organs, explore the abdominal cavity. The intestinal loops are held aside with a metal clamp to give a better view of all the structures supplying the stomach with blood. There is fresh blood in the abdominal cavity, a sign of a major internal injury.

'Dammit, this blood must be coming from somewhere,' mutters the surgeon.

After a careful search, he discovers a tear at the root of the intestine.

A curved needle fixed to a long holder is handed to him. A ligature is applied to the bleeding vessels. The operation is over. Now it is the assistant's job to close the abdominal cavity.

I lie there, covered up, staring at the bandages on my hands.

I feel so lonely. Has anyone noticed I'm missing? Probably not. It's just too silly. He has to abduct me on the last day at work just before my holiday. I needn't worry about the cat, my neighbour will look after her. What a stupid coincidence that I met her on the stairs on Friday morning! I told her then about my week off, and said I'd have to leave in a hurry after work if I wanted to catch my flight to the south. She's often looked after the cat before. She'll be a little surprised that I didn't look in to say goodbye, but she won't think much of it. So no one will realize I'm missing until next week, if at all. And suppose I'm still not back the week after next? Who knows, the boss may think I've carried out my threat to look for a new job. I've said I'm going to give notice often enough. Whenever I was infuriated about something I'd say, 'If I can find something else I'll be out of here tomorrow!' They probably won't even ask where I am at the office.

They still have Lilli to do all the work and save the boss my salary. Not that he'll save much that way, it's not exactly lavish. Lilli and I run the whole show. We do everything; we're secretaries, car salesmen, gardeners, cleaning ladies rolled into one. We even change spark plugs and do oil changes when there's a shortage of mechanics. The boss certainly can't complain about us, and a little more money a month would be only fair. At the moment business isn't so good, but not really bad either. I know the figures. And if he doesn't like to do it officially, I'd be happy for him to slip us a little of the money he's made under the counter himself. At least I wouldn't have to pay tax on it.

He really exploits Lilli, she does literally everything for him. She even sleeps with him. What good is that going to do her? The boss is never going to leave his wife and children, however often he promises her he will. I don't know what Lilli sees in him. He's fat, he has a bald patch, he's married and his kids are a couple of spoilt brats.

His fiftieth birthday was two weeks ago – he celebrated in a big way with all the staff. He really splashed out and invited us all to the Japanese restaurant. I have to admit it was fun. A buffet of cold food in tiny portions washed down with rice wine isn't really to my taste, too chilly and slippery, but at least it was fish, it wasn't meat. And the atmosphere was good, and since we were having a good time he wanted to go on to the disco with Lilli and me.

On the way home he kept putting his hand on my knee. He was rather drunk. He got more outspoken when he said goodnight. 'Call me Rüdiger, Monika, do.' And then he made me a very explicit offer. I went bright red and could have sunk into the ground with shame. Not for the world!

Sometimes he's really repulsive. He's the one who ought to be stuck here, not me. After all, it's the boss who has the key to the safe, and here I am in the shit.

Hans wanted me to give him the key when he attacked me at the garage. Is he still after the money? You bet he is. He didn't just want his revenge on me, he wanted the money from the safe as well.

The money from the safe. Why not? Why not nick it? The boss has been exploiting me for years, messing me about. I'd only be taking the proper salary he didn't pay me. And giving him a bit of a fright into the bargain. I'll have him grovelling on the floor and whining. 'Please, please don't hurt me.' I like that thought. I can already see the red patches he always gets on his face when he's worked up. Could there be a better chance than this of paying him out?

Hans can do the dirty work and I'll get the money. Hans will play along, I'm sure he will. He'll do anything to get his hands on the cash. He doesn't want his revenge on me any more, or he'd have taken it long ago, I'm sure of that too. He's looking after me, he's concerned for me. He was always easy to manage, why wouldn't I be able to handle him now? What's to stop me? With him in tow I'm unbeatable. He's my tool, my weapon.

'Think about it, Monika, and if you'd like to, well, give me a call.' Those were my boss's parting remarks in the car when we said goodnight. Well, I have thought about it. I'm going to call you, Rüdiger darling!

Hans comes upstairs. He's carrying a tray with two mugs of coffee, a carton of milk, and some cheese sandwiches. The coffee smells good. Exactly what I need now. I sit up on the bed.

'Coffee?'

She gets off the bed, sits down at the table with me. I push one of the mugs of coffee her way, put her cheese sandwich down beside it. I've cut it into little pieces, the way my mother always cut things up for me when I was little. She cut bread into fingers, and each finger was a train ready to drive into the station, and the station was my mouth.

'Like me to feed you?' She nods, smiles at me.

I pick up finger after finger of the cheese sandwich and put it in her mouth. She chews, and starts talking even with her mouth full. 'Suppose we get the money from that safe together?'

At first I don't understand, I've no idea what she's talking about. The money? But she doesn't have the key. I searched her clothes.

She goes on smiling at me.

Tilting her head slightly, she looks at me. I sit there, I don't say a word. After a while she asks, 'Why haven't you taken me back?'

'I don't know. I wanted you to stay here.' I look at her, look into her eyes.

We sit there in silence, and I feed her with fingers of cheese sandwich and help her to sip the hot coffee.

'So what do you think, shall we go and get the key now? And then get the money out of the safe?'

Well, why not? This whole thing has gone off course from the start, but if she can help me to lay my hands on the money now...and after that we'll see. I wait another minute, keep her guessing, then I say, 'How are you going to get hold of the key?' I'm curious to know what she's thought up.

'My boss always keeps the key in the inside pocket of his jacket.'

'And how do we get at his jacket?'

'He fancies me, I know that. I'll call him and tell him to come here. Then I'll distract his attention, you can knock him down and take the key. We'll do it today, then we'll have all night to empty the safe and clear out.'

I sit there listening to her plan. It's rather vague, but I don't have a better one, so why not? I've nothing to lose. I rub my chin, think it over. 'You think that will work?'

'Let's just try it. Then we'll know if it works or not.'

I think for a moment longer, and then I bring the flat of my hand down on the table.

'Right, then let's try it, darling.'

She looks at me with a mixture of disbelief and astonishment. You can positively see her thinking feverishly. There, my love, you weren't expecting me to be so easily persuaded to go along with your plan!

'Darling...?

'Do you have thirty pfennigs? We can drive to the nearest telephone box.'

I'm not your darling. You've got my brother on your conscience, you bastard. You're going to help me grab that money and get my boss off my back, that's all. Payback time!

'Let's go!'

He goes ahead. I follow him. Of my own free will! I keep my hands stretched out in front of me so as not to catch myself on the thorns.

It's a tight fit in the phone box. He gives me a kiss on the shoulder. At least I think he kissed my shoulder. I felt his lips, anyway. Oh, drop that!

'Dial 68 75 99, then you can hold the receiver to my ear.' Hans does everything I tell him.

'Hello, Rüdiger, it's me. Moni.'

And then I start talking. I've been thinking about us a lot these last few days, I say, about him and me. I thought it all through again. I lay the charm on thick. I tell him it was wrong of me to say no, but he has to understand that I simply didn't trust myself. I go on soft-soaping him over the phone. I say I'd like our relationship to be something really special. Something that belongs just to us. I talk and talk, carry on about being careful because after all he has a wife and children, and I wouldn't like there to be any gossip among our colleagues. But in the last few days I haven't been able to think of anything else, only him. That's why I've plucked up all my courage and I'm calling him now. I ramble on and on. My voice sounds totally strange to me, I'm cooing, I'm all lovey-dovey. I hear myself asking if he couldn't come and meet me. 'I mean now, before my courage deserts me again.' I tell him I've found a little place hidden away – 'All for you and me.' It would be the ideal place, no one would ever find out about it. We'd be all alone there, just the two of us. I chat him up, I flirt, in the end I almost forget to tell him where to go. 'Oh yes, the address…wait a minute, do you have a pen there?' I describe the way, explaining very patiently where he has to turn off the road and follow the track through the forest until he can't drive any further. I tell him he can leave his car behind a Fiesta that he'll see there, and I tell him the way past the pond and over to the mill. I'd be waiting for him there, I say. 'Oh and please don't be alarmed. I've bandaged my hands up because I fell off my bike,' I say, but I can tell him that story later, when he's with me.

At a sign from me, Hans hangs up.

Right. Now for Part Two of the plan.

Hans smelt my hair when I came out of the phone box. I must stink pretty bad by now, but he seems to like the smell of me.

Keep him on the boil, you still need him. The game is just beginning, and I'm almost enjoying it.

I push down the door handle to the phone box, hold the door open, let her go in first. She couldn't have managed the door herself with her bandaged hands. Coming out, she presses close to me. Her hair comes close to my face. I'd never have thought you could pull that trick off with your boss so well, girlie! Hats off to you, still waters run deep. I was standing beside her while she rabbited on and on, talking like a waterfall. She really chatted up that guy at the other end of the line. Turned him on. I could see she was enjoying all this more and more. Talking herself into a fine state.

But back at the mill, she can hardly bear the pain. I noticed in the car how the painkilling effect was gradually wearing off. Now I can see it in her face. She is turning paler all the time, her features are more and more convulsed.

'My hands hurt again. You must give me another injection!'

'Better not. Your head won't be clear, you could mess this whole thing up!'

'Please! It hurts horribly. I can't stand it. Please do something, help me!'

Reluctantly, I fill a syringe and pull the plunger up, because with the pain she's no use to me either. The way she looks now, that guy wouldn't fancy her at all. It takes exactly the right dose to control the pain. Well, she doesn't have to seduce him, just entice him here and then distract his attention, that'll do. I'll deal with the rest, because her boss will never fall into her honey-trap, not the way she looks. I have to think up some idea or we might as well say goodbye to the whole plan. Slowly, I press the plunger down in the syringe. I hope she's not had too much.

The wave runs through my body again, there's a tingling in my stomach, it's nice. The pain ebbs away bit by bit, from wrist to fingers. Finally it reaches somewhere in the region of my fingertips and then disappears entirely.

I'm ready now, he can come now, my little boss. I lie on the bed in readiness. I don't have to wait long. Footsteps on the lower floor. That can only be darling Rüdiger. He's in a real hurry to get here.

Hans has hidden outside and is waiting for my signal. Rüdiger enters the room behind the metal door. It's so quiet that I can hear every one of his footsteps. Now he's on the stairs below me. The first step creaks. I feel rather queasy. Pull yourself together, no going back now, only forward.

At each of his steps the wooden stairs creak and groan. Then a pause. The noise they make probably scares him. He must be looking around, maybe he feels a bit unsure of himself.

'Rüdiger, I'm up here, waiting for you.'

That works. He comes trudging up. First his face appears. Greasy hair combed back. I feel I weigh very little, I could grin and giggle the whole time. I hope I don't muck this up.

With difficulty, he makes his way up through the trap-door. Oops – on the last step he seems to stumble, catches himself just in time. I put my bandaged hand in front of my mouth. Mustn't burst out laughing now!

Rüdiger turns to look for me. It's not a human head on his massive body now, he looks like a fat pig. With a snout in the middle of his face. Curious, surprised, I stand up and stare at him. This can't be true! He comes towards me, and as he comes closer his face keeps changing all the time. He looks at me out of two little round piggy eyes. His lower jaw is jutting, he seems to be grinning, and two mighty tusks come into sight. The little piggy eyes wander restlessly back and forth, searching the room. Searching it for a rival.

'There's no one here, only you and me.'

The pig snuffles in my direction, the hair on the back of

its neck standing up. It comes towards me, its head rocking this way and that. Coming closer and closer. Pigs don't see well, they rely on their snuffling noses to explore their surroundings. Its nose is right in front of my face. That snout is almost black, wet and shining, moving all the time. The pig breathes in deeply, then breathes out with a loud snort, a disgusting smell of carrion surrounds me.

I think the animal's very excited. To soothe it, I run my thickly padded hand gently over the bristly hairs on the back of its neck. They look like thin black wires. I can't feel the bristles through the thick bandaging, I can only see that they're standing up, and they hardly give way at all under the pressure of my hand.

The pig's little eyes sparkle at me. It snorts. The curving, dagger-like tusks are much too big for its mouth. They push the top lip up. The pig looks as if it is baring its teeth.

I'm afraid of the animal. The pig snorts several times in succession. It grabs me. I fight it off as well as I can. It stares angrily at me. I'm so frightened I can't move. Hell, where on earth is Hans? The animal stops for a moment, seems sorry for me. Then it flings its massive body against the table. The table shoots to one side and crashes into the wardrobe.

The pig stands in front of me now, getting bigger, more

than a head taller than me. I'm still standing there, I can't do anything but stare at its great tusks. It's foaming at the mouth. A slimy thread of saliva hangs down, gradually lengthening, comes loose and drops to the floor. Time seems to stand still.

I cautiously take a small step back. The pig puts its head slightly on one side. I must get out of here, I must get away from this beast, quick! Another step back. The bed is right behind me, I collide with it, can't keep on my feet, I fall full length on the mattress.

The pig flings itself on me. I close my eyes, feel its weight on me, its hot breath on my neck. Its damp slobber drops on my cheek, runs on to my lips.

I can hardly move, it's like a ton weight on top of me. I turn my head aside, open my eyes. Hans's head appears in the opening of the trapdoor. I gasp for air, the body is so heavy lying on me. I shout as loud as I can. 'Do something, this pig is raping me!'

The head disappears again.

'No, no, you can't go away. Help me, stick this pig!'

The pig is trying to force my thighs apart. I resist with all my might, I tense my buttocks. I don't want this. It can't do this, it's an animal, it can't do this.

Slobber runs along my neck, down to my breasts. I feel

that moist snout everywhere, on my face, in my hair.

'Hans, stick the pig, stick the pig!'

I see Hans coming up through the trapdoor with a long, silvery, gleaming knife in his hand.

The pig howls. The pressure between my thighs relaxes. Why doesn't Hans help me to push the pig off? I turn, trying to wriggle out from under it.

The pig falls, turns on its own axis as it falls and crashes to the wooden floor. There's blood everywhere, spurting and pumping out of the opened body. Guts spill out of the belly, fall squelching to the floor, spread there. I feel sick. Everything's white and blurred, everything's floating in the air.

I open my eyes and see that wooden ceiling again. I'm used to it by now. And to the sickness. It must be something to do with the injection.

I'm afraid to sit up. The dead pig must be lying beside the bed. Half human, half animal. I look round, everything's the same as usual. A dream? There are gleaming dark patches on the floor, someone's been using a wet mop on it. Is it real, then? The pig was here and Hans got rid of it?

Nonsense, there's no such thing as a half-human, half-animal hybrid.

I stand up, climb down the wooden stairs. It's difficult

without any help. I can't hold on to anything with my thick mittens of bandaging.

Hans is just coming up the steps from the cellar.

'What happened, Hans?'

Bloody hell, I knew it, the whole thing went wrong. The way she was, I might have known she had no idea what she was doing. I chucked the body down the stairs. He was bleeding like a pig. Blood everywhere. What else could I have done? She was in the process of botching it all up. She wasn't capable of reasonable action any more. I'd hidden downstairs. The guy wasn't up the stairs yet before I heard her shrill, hysterical laughter from above. I stole up the stairs after him and found the poor fellow standing in front of her, baffled, trying to soothe her somehow. Then, when he tried to take hold of her, she went right round the bend. Screaming her head off. Yelling the whole time. And then it all happened very fast. The guy turned round. When he saw me he realized what was going on. Understood at once that he'd been lured into a trap. He didn't hang about, he went straight for me. Grabbed hold of me. He was at least a head taller than me, a real colossus. What was I to do? I had no choice, I simply stuck the knife into him without stopping to think.

It was like back then with Father.

How Father yelled at me, flung himself on me. He'd been boozing. The old man wanted to kill me. He was dead drunk, he didn't even know I was his son. Didn't know he was going for his own flesh and blood.

So I stabbed, twice, three times. I can't remember any more. My old man survived the whole thing. They saved his rotten life with an emergency operation. And they locked me up. What happened to my old man I've no idea, couldn't care less. He'll have drunk himself to death, what else?

But no emergency operation is going to help that great bag of lard now. No one can do anything for him. I dragged him down to the bunker. Threw his keys and valuables on the bed. Put the guy himself in a plastic sack and then cleaned everything up.

I'm on my way up from the bunker when she comes downstairs. Looks terrible, white as a sheet. Somehow she manages to support herself on the stairs with her bandaged hands. Swaying alarmingly at every step. She stares at me as if I am death in person.

'What happened, Hans?'

'I'll tell you later.'

I don't feel like explanations now. There's no time, either. Doesn't she realize we have to get away? Now we've done *that* we're really in the shit.

'What happened, Hans?'

Why does she keep banging on about this Hans?

'My name's Dimitri, not Hans!'

'Why not Hans? But you *are* Hans.'

Why on earth would I be Hans? She's looking at me incredulously.

'But what you did when you...'

What does she mean? What am I supposed to have done?

'But surely you're...Where did you live as a child?'

Can't the silly cow get it into her head that this is no time for playing games? Keep calm. Shouting at her does no good.

'If you must know, I was born in Naila, we lived here, there and everywhere. My mother died, I spent time in homes, my father was a jailbird and a drunk. Satisfied now?'

All of a sudden she's perfectly quiet, looks even paler. Bends her head, looks at her bandaged hands.

I look at my bandaged hands. Everything's going round and round in my head. I can hardly form a clear thought. My heart is racing. Keep calm, try to keep perfectly calm.

'Why were you in my apartment?'

'I was watching you.'

Does his face distort into a slight smile when he says that?

'Why did you take the photo of me and my brother?'

He looks at me, the smile is gone. His voice is impatient, he's obviously all on edge.

'That little boy's your brother? I might have known it. The picture reminded me of something, that's all.'

I close my eyes. It's all black. Now what? Think! He isn't Hans. That makes everything different. He didn't know

Joachim at all, he had nothing to do with him. He's a total stranger. A kidnapper. A criminal. A murderer.

I know what I have to do.

I'm freezing. I have to get out of here. Out! Out!

Damn it, damn it, don't just stand here wailing! Try to remember! Try to remember! I hit my face with the flat of my hand, strike my head. Remember when Father was building this bunker for an air-raid shelter. 'Air-raid shelter' – I ask you! He was always drivelling on about the bunker. As a child he told me he'd been buried in rubble during the War. He had to dig his way out of the ruins with a tin mug and his bare hands. A man who'd been buried too, along with him and my grandmother, had helped them, he said.

He changed the story every time he told it. The old air-raid warden turned into a soldier, the soldier became an expert on hand-to-hand fighting, a hero. His own part in the story kept getting bigger and more heroic as well. He talked about the bright light that met them when they finally dug themselves out. In my imagination I could see them with bloodstained weals on their hands, dirt under their fingernails, sweat.

Only much later did I realize that the story was a pack of lies from beginning to end, like most of his stories. He wasn't even three in May 1945, he couldn't have experienced those events.

All the same, he was talking about the bunker the whole time – he insisted on calling it that. A shelter, a kitchen, a bedroom. With the old furniture we'd thrown out.

He thought of a way to get a water supply in. Pumping up water from the well was no problem, but what about the outlet for the waste water? The pipe led straight into the stream. I had to help him dig out the place for it. This 'brilliant idea' led to the collapse of the stream bed and the complete flooding of the shelter in the bunker. It took us weeks to get everything sealed. We put thick concrete tanking on the bed of the stream to secure it, and repaired the concrete wall of the central kitchen area of the bunker, which had mostly been carried away, using brickwork. We filled the space in between with the old tiles from the roof, most of them broken, which had been stored in the cellar before.

Then he decided to do without a proper water outlet and a toilet, said a large hollow space with gravel under the kitchen area would have to do. He was a great one for changing his plans. He probably didn't believe there was going to be a real air raid, the bunker business was just an excuse. He wanted a hiding place where he could go if one of his many business deals blew up in his face. He always had something on the boil. Sometimes he had plenty of cash, sometimes he was broke, always looking for the great coup, the big one, the deal of his life...he traded in anything and everything, like smuggled cigarettes. Went around making out he was a gas-meter reader, an advertising agent for newspapers, an insurance broker. He was a loser, always on the verge of jail. Air-raid shelter, talk about ridiculous!

The air supply was another great fiasco. He fiddled about with that for a long time; none of his ideas looked like being really successful. A proper ventilation system would have cost a lot of money, and he wasn't willing to pay out for it. Finally he decided on always leaving the door into the cellar just a crack open. The simplest ideas are usually the best; who would think of climbing down a dark, slippery passage in the cellar of an old mill? That was him all over, never did anything properly, his ideas were silly in the first place and he always left them half done.

And now here I am in the shit. Talk about an idiot. I only wanted to pick up the key to the safe, then get the money and go. Now what?

The door to the cellar is closed. From inside it can't be opened except with its key, and its key is in the other side, damn it. Every breath I take is using up air. Who knows how long it will hold out? Well, if necessary there's always the narrow crack under the door.

I slowly straighten up and grope my way over to the iron door. The surface feels cold and rough. I slip my fingers over the flaking paint, the rusty patches, until I'm standing upright. My whole body is stiff, it hurts. Keeping my fingertips on the metal, I turn to the room. I feel the door behind me. In this total darkness I've completely lost my sense of direction. The door behind me is my safety anchor. I overcome my fears, step into the darkness, take small tripping steps in what I think is the direction of the entrance to the kitchen area. If I couldn't feel the ground under my feet I wouldn't know which way was up and which was down. I open my eyes wide, although they're not the slightest use to me. Step by step, heel to toe. One foot after another, don't panic, keep calm, don't panic. Where's that bloody wall? The room can't be that big. Oh, shit! I put my arms right out ahead of me, my fingertips feel the door frame, run along it slowly, thoughtfully. Keep calm, don't panic. This is the door frame, through here and I'm in the kitchen.

Just to my left is the little kitchen counter; I feel my way along it. The fittings. As well as the bad air supply, water could be a problem. No one's used this place for years, Father least of all. The bunker didn't do him much good, no air raid, and what did he get instead? Years in jail for theft and crimes of violence, as they so delicately put it in official language. He was violent and no mistake. Particularly to Mother. Not that that was what put him in jail. On my sixth birthday he beat Mother half to death. Hit her in the face repeatedly. At first she held her hands in front of her, then she gave up, which didn't stop Father hitting her again and again. Always in the face and always with his clenched fist. Until her eyebrows were bleeding, her eyes swollen, her lips thick as your finger. I can't remember any reason. There probably wasn't one.

He disappeared for a few days, we were glad of that. On Mother's instructions I dabbed her face with cold water. But it became more and more distorted, turned into a face like a clown's – I can't help laughing when I think of it. Here I am in the shit, laughing myself silly over something that's not funny at all. I'm the same kind of idiot and loser as Father.

I turn on the tap. A mixture of water and air splashes out.

More air than water, because soon there's only a trickle, then drops, then no more. Right, so I'll have to go thirsty. The air seems to be holding out. There ought to be food in the cupboard. A few years ago I opened one of those gleaming cans. Pumpernickel. It was dry but edible. I grope for the door of the kitchen cupboard. Open it. Don't knock your head on the door. Cautiously reach in. In this darkness every move I make is slower, more hesitant. I stretch, literally. Right at the back there are still some cans. Including small ones – there ought to be meat in those. I shake the tap, it drips again. I hit it, the dripping gets stronger. A cup under it. I need a cup or a glass. Here. I feel the cup with both hands, then the tap. It all takes time, I just hope the dripping won't stop. There, done it! I wait, count the drops. Can't concentrate, keep beginning again. The sound of the drops of water changes as more water falls into the cup. I dip my forefinger in to see how full the cup is. Half full. I take it in both hands, carry it to my mouth, sip – it tastes stale, but I drink it. Another little victory. I won't die of thirst. Hey, Father, I'm not such a loser as you after all! Take a look this way, wherever you may be now! Arsehole!

I lean against the sink and look into the darkness. Arsehole myself! Idiot! If only I'd taken the key out of the other side of the cellar door I wouldn't be here now. I wouldn't be trapped in this bunker. Something has to happen. I slowly feel my way back to the iron door. I brace myself against it, push, shake it. The damn door is riddled with rust, but I can't get it to give way. No luck! I kick it until my toes hurt, again and again, again and again. I'm not giving up.

But I'm thirsty again, so back to the sink, faster this time. I'm already getting used to the darkness, I feel more secure. Just a little push against the door frame and I'm in the kitchen. Take the cup again in both hands, carefully. Don't spill anything. Drink. Now I need the loo. There, now across the room to the toilet. Your work too, Father. Toilet, that's a good one – just an earth closet! I hope I won't piss myself. That's all I need. The jet of urine hits the gravel, splashing amongst the stones.

Back to the cup, drink, over to the door, lie down on the bed. All going well so far. Only how do I get out of here? I can't think of anything else, always the same: how do I get out of here? Getting help from outside, shouting or screaming – no, ridiculous. I try it all the same. I shout and shout, so loud that my ears hurt, there's an echo in them, then a deathly hush, quieter than silence itself. I'm buried alive, my life's not worth a bean. Bloody hell, I'll never get out of here!

The door! I have to break the lock of the iron door open.

I stand up, go into the kitchen, feel about for the drawer, pull it open. Get it right out. It falls to the floor, the cutlery clatters. I kneel down, feel the contents lying on the ground. Try to fish out a piece of wire, or something like wire. There, sharp, long, flexible. I go over to the door, colliding with several obstacles in my way. I feel the metal door with one hand to find the lock. At last! I manage to get my chosen tool into the opening. The key is in the door on the outside, so I'll have to push it out and then pick the lock of the door. But I can't shift the key. Bloody hell!

I hit the wall with my fists, I can't take any more. I turn round, let myself slip to the floor with my back to the wall. I begin to cry. I sit there like a little kid, knees drawn up, hands in front of my face, crying.

The wall. The bloody wall. I must get through the wall.

Get through the wall, but how?

I see myself going into the kitchen, walking carefully. Like in one of those action movies I've watched dozens of times. Only this time I'm the hero in the paramilitary boots and army jacket. I take my jacket off. Run both hands over my short hair. I reach for the heavy gold chain round my neck, carry the cross to my mouth and kiss it. After that I put one leg against the wall, at an angle. Take three long, slow, strong breaths. Fix my eyes on the little bit of wall next to the kitchen counter. I push off from the wall with a war cry, shoulder turned to it. The wall breaks with a deafening noise. Bright light comes in through the opening.

Or that's how it's supposed to go. Pull yourself together, you're the hero. I wipe the tears and snot from my face with the back of my hand, stand up. Desperately I beat my fists on the wall until my knuckles hurt. I go on hitting it, again and again, kicking it, hitting it with the palm of my hand... just a faint slapping sound. Damn. In my rage and disappointment I prop myself flat against the wall with both hands. Push my head against it until my nose meets its hardness with a loud crack. The pain makes its way inside me. I'm numbed, I lose my balance and let myself fall to the floor again. My nose is swelling and warm blood drips on my hand. The wall stands there, firm and immovable. I'm in a dungeon.

In my rage I go on hitting the wall. A clear, slapping sound. It sounds different just here...test it again. Yes, it does sound different!

Cautiously, I knock against the whole wall with my right hand, from bottom to top and back again. The sound changes, it's a duller, darker note at the top. What sounds duller, darker? Bricks! The top half of the wall is bricks. The solution, that's the solution! There's no getting through concrete, but bricks I can deal with! Quick! Mustn't lose any time. I crouch down, feel the floor for tools I could use, as sharp and pointed as possible. Knife, scissors, fork.

I stand up, hack at the wall as hard as I can. Clench my hand into a fist and hold my tools firmly. The scissors are the easiest to grip. I hack and hack until I hear the plaster flaking away, first in small crumbs, then in larger pieces. I keep feeling the part I've uncovered. The sweat starts running down my body. I don't give up, I scrape and scratch with the scissors, the knife and fork, until I can feel joints between the bricks. Yes, they're bricks all right, I've won!

I hack, scrape, thrust until my whole arm is throbbing with pain. My fingers are sore, they hurt like hell. But one of the bricks is already moving, shifting slightly. I need a lever. Damn it, I need a lever! The long, steel, the knife-sharpener! I could use that as a lever! I search the floor for it. There it is! With all my might, I put the steel to the joint and the brick shifts more and more, its neighbours start wobbling as well. One of the joints is damp, presumably from my sweat; I was leaning against the wall to get a better grip. I'm sweating like a pig.

Go on working, you must go on working! Why is the floor suddenly wet? I feel the wall. It's wet too. The brick in the middle is wobbling. By shaking it I loosen it until I can pull it a little way out. I can hear the bricks grating against each other. They slip, they get caught against one another. I try to loosen the brick entirely. My fingers can't get a good purchase, they keep slipping off. I have almost no strength left. With the very last of it, I tug at the brick and it suddenly comes away. Holding it, I stumble back into the room, fall and lie on my back. Hell! I'm lying in a puddle. Everything's wet, the whole floor. I run my fingers back and forth in the wetness. Cold water, my trousers and shirt are drenched, everything's sticking to my skin, unpleasant damp cold behind me.

It's splashing! I jump up, two steps to the wall. My hands touch it, feel the water coming in. It's flowing, streaming in!

Shit! Shit! The stream! Now I have to work really fast or the bunker will be flooded. Like all that time ago, it will be flooded right out and I'll drown miserably.

I shake the bricks, haul one after another out of the wall. Water and mud flood in. More and more water and mud. The water rises fast, I can feel it's already up to my ankles. I reach into the hole I've made. There's a space behind the wall. I grope around, feel upwards, nothing there as far as I can go.

I brace myself, force myself head first through the hole in the wall; my arms feel the mud, try to find the ground below.

Nothing solid, just cold swampy stuff. I haul myself up with all my might, lift my leg over the wall, still no solid ground. Hell, I have to try it! Shoulder first, I fling myself into the muddy void. Keep my mouth shut, hold my breath. Close my eyes. My head is sucked into the slippery ooze. I'm sinking deeper in. Slowly, I paddle my arms and legs against the mud. The swamp gets heavier and heavier the deeper I go. Slowly, without meaning to, I roll over on my back. I get more and more lethargic. It's like moving in slow motion. Or no, I'm not moving myself, the mud is rolling me over and moving me. I'm caught like a turtle lying on its back. In a minute or so I'll be unconscious, a few minutes more and I'll be dead. All perfectly simple. My mind is strangely clear. It works slowly, but it's clear.

Dead! I deserve it. I've killed a man. I see that mistreated, pale body, stab wounds all over, lying beside the bed. My vision moves away, the corpse gets smaller, I see the whole room, brightly lit by the paraffin lamps. Someone is hunched on a chair, I can't see who. It's a woman. Face hidden in her hands, head on her knees. I move further away still, see the roof of the mill, in need of repair, the forest, it all goes dark and quiet.

A bang. I open my eyes. Thick, black fluid gets in under the lids. I close them again. Gurgling and rumbling above me. Solid bits of something sink down on me through the viscous, jelly-like mush where I'm caught. Stones and earth? I want to open my mouth, scream, breathe! My wish for air gets stronger all the time. I want to breathe. Air! Hold out! Don't do it! It's like in the swimming pool when whoever comes up first has lost.

Another crashing sound, dull but loud. I roll around, turn, am turned, my left arm is caught up somewhere, comes free again. I roll over, I'm pushed. I lie where I am.

I'm breathing. Breathing in and out, slowly, deeply.

I'm alive! I'm still alive. I open my eyes. I blink. There's a huge hole in the wall opposite me, glaring light. Narrowing my eyes, I look around. Debris, mud, gooey stuff. My left shoulder hurts. Otherwise I'm all right, I can move my hands and feet, all there and movable.

I get to my feet. Rubble and debris all over the place. Through my narrowed eyes, it looks as if the beams of light are falling in through the hole in the wall. A pleasant, warm feeling flows through me, I'm happy. Happy to be still alive.

I make for the hole, slip on slimy stones, trudge through muddy water, clamber over the rest of the wall and out into the open.

Above me, streaks of cloud in a blue-grey sky. A huge crater beside the mill. I climb over the side wall, which falls away at a shallow incline. Go around the barn. The iron door to the mill is closed.

I go over to it, brace myself as hard as I can against the door. Open it. She's sitting on the floor in the back part of the room. The room is dark, the paraffin lamps must have gone out long ago. She looks up, sees me, can't take it in. Sits there without moving, just stares at me. The knife is lying on one of the shelves near the door. I reach blindly for it, without looking. Slowly, she stands up, doesn't take her eyes off me. I go towards her. When I'm very close to her I stop. She looks at me. I can feel her breath on my face. She'd have left me to die in the bunker like a filthy, lousy rat. I reach for the back of her neck with my left hand, feel her hair in my hand. Lean a little way down to her as I thrust with my right hand. She's looking into my eyes all the time.

Police cars, fire engine, engines running, noise. The entrance to the mill is brightly illuminated by strong floodlights.

Glaring artificial light inside the place too. On the floor an injured woman, bleeding profusely. The emergency doctor kneels on the floor beside his patient, swiftly tending her wounds. Trying to stop the bleeding with wound compresses and pressure bandages.

The paramedics are ready with the stretcher.

'She's stabilized now. You can take her away. Don't worry, looks worse than it is. She'll make it.' The emergency doctor stands up, leaves the woman to the paramedics, who carefully place her on the stretcher.

Access to the cellar is secured by the police with red and

white tape. A uniformed officer stands beside this barrier waiting for his colleagues from the police records department. There's a corpse in a plastic sack in the back room of the cellar.